The Stars Are Upside Down

Tavy had spent her only savings on the £5-passage to Australia and felt exhilarated by the sense of space around her. Neither the rough overland journey to her destination, nor even the lecherous attempts of drunken Willie Moser, could weaken her determination to make a success of her new job.

When she at last reaches the Campion property, however, she finds hidden tensions beneath the affluent surface. There's the cool but kindly Mistress, sadly yearning for her English home; bored and spiteful Louisa, always ready for a sneering comment; and arrogant Harry, her brother, used to having his own way.

But what most occupies Tavy are her secret visits to the hut of the rough bushman, Jake, to look after his baby, Joe. Knowing that the Campions want Jake off the land, Tavy's visits become more and more risky, until events reach a dramatic and shattering climax . . .

Also available in Fontana Lions

Gabriel Alington

The Stars Are Upside Down

FONTANA · LIONS

First published in Great Britain 1980
by William Heinemann Ltd.
First published in Fontana Lions 1982
by William Collins Sons & Co Ltd
14 St James's Place, London SW1

© Gabriel Alington 1980

Printed in Great Britain
by William Collins Sons & Co Ltd, Glasgow

To Diana, without whom . . .

Chapter One

Tavy stood at the deck rail staring out across the sea. There was a light in the distance. She could see it winking on the far horizon where the shadowed water met the sky. Towards evening, the wind had freshened, driving great plumes of cloud from the west. It filled the sails of the *Henrietta* so that she picked up speed and surged ahead as if she too was impatient to reach harbour.

"Look, a light!" Someone else had seen it too.

"Where?"

"A light! Where?"

Other passengers hurried to the side.

"See, over there. It blinks on and off."

There was a heavy step from behind.

"That'll be Macquarie Lighthouse on the South Head."

Tavy recognised the voice. It was Duggan, one of the crew, a big friendly sailor with a bushy beard. "How far away is it?" she asked him.

"What's that?" He peered at her in the darkness. "Oh, it's you, little lady. Well, hard to say exact like — twenty-five miles, thirty maybe."

"When will we be there?"

"Early morning if this wind keeps up."

"Oh!" Tavy drew her breath. She could hardly believe it. At last, after over four months at sea, they were nearly there.

"Did you hear? He said we'd be there in the morning!"

1

The excitement spread.

"Tomorrow morning!"

"We're nearly there, nearly in Sydney!"

"Tomorrow we'll be in Australia!"

Nearly there. Nearly there. The words went on in Tavy's head to the rhythmic creaking of the ship. She lay in her upper berth, watching the shadows from the candle lanterns glide across the deckhead, listening to the restless sounds of the 107 emigrant women and children sleeping round her. Some, like Tavy, were single girls in search of work, adventure, a husband. Others were married women, their husbands segregated in the male accommodation, with children and babies, three born on the voyage. They hoped for a run of land, a house of their own, a chance for their children. All of them dreamed of a happier, more prosperous life than the one they had left behind as they tossed and murmured through the night. More than the noise, Tavy hated the lack of air, the stuffy heat of the lower deck, the smells of stale food, tobacco, vomit and sweat mingled with the stench of the latrine buckets wafting in from the washroom. It was worst when the weather was rough, when heavy seas sweeping over the ship made it unsafe to go on deck. At first when they had met a storm, Tavy had struggled to get out, desperate for fresh air, not knowing that the hatches were battened down. It had been Duggan who had found her at the top of the steps as he brought down provisions from the galley.

"Please," she had begged, "please let me go outside."

"Let you out! More than my life's worth," Duggan had told her. "You'd be overboard in no time, a little snip like you!"

"I'll hang on. I'll stay near the mast," she had pleaded, clutching Duggan as the ship lurched sideways. "Oh, please, I feel sick."

But it was no use. Duggan was adamant and Tavy, who never gave in without a battle, felt too ill to resist. She had allowed Duggan to help her back to the lower deck. The storm wouldn't last long, besides she'd soon get her sea-legs. Best thing was to have something to eat, felt worse if you were empty. A good plate of stew and she'd be fine.

That had finished Tavy. She had vomited continually, retching violently, her body contorted like twisted wire. She had never known that sickness could be so overpowering. Even sips of water from kind Annie Button, the Yorkshire girl who slept below her, brought on another attack. Finally, drained of all her strength, she had lain in her berth for days, weeks — she had lost all sense of time — her thoughts a muddle of memories and dreams. Half waking to the cry of children's voices, she was back at Saint Agatha's helping Aunt Lavender in the junior dormitory. Dear Aunt Lavender in her white lace cap, gathering her orphaned charges into her plump embrace, loving each one from the youngest junior to Lumpity Willy, who was fully grown with a big awkward body and the mind of a baby.

Tavy could not remember a time when she had not lived in the shabby brick house in Barrington Street, with 'Saint Agatha's Orphanage' painted above the front door. All she knew of her past was that she had been left there before her second birthday by her father, with five gold sovereigns in a small leather purse, and that she had been named Octavia Mary after her mother who had died giving birth to Tavy, her only child. For over twelve years, Saint Agatha's had been Tavy's home. It was crowded, noisy and spartan but, although they were all expected to work hard and help, Aunt Lavender's charges were happy enough. There was a sense of security in the strict daily routine, which only varied at Christmas or Easter or on special occasions such as the time ten years ago when the young Queen had married her handsome Prince Albert. Tavy was only five then, but she could remember it vividly; the bustle and excitement as they walked in a crocodile from Pimlico to Knightsbridge, standing on tiptoe and not being able to see anything except the backs of the people in front of her. And the flags. She had looked up and seen them, flapping in the wind, gaily coloured with golden tassels. And she had looked beyond them at the sky far, far away above the roofs. It was misty and pale and went on for ever and all through the day, while the processions and pageantry went on around her, she had kept on tilting her head back to stare at the sky. Then, because even the youngest were allowed to stay up late, it had grown quite dark and Tavy had seen a star. There was just one at first, a pinprick of light, but then she saw another and another till they seemed to pop out everywhere. That was what Tavy remembered best. After that, she often used to stare at the sky, specially at night when there might be a star, though too often they were hidden behind clouds and fog. Increasingly as she grew older, she longed to be on her own. Sometimes she would stand and stretch her arms wide, just to see if she could, and more and more she watched the sky because in her crowded life only there was there space and quietness.

"Brooding again," Aunt Lavender would chide, catching her with her nose pressed against the dormitory window.

"I'm not brooding," Tavy would reply indignantly. "I was just looking . . ."

"That will do, Octavia."

It was no use trying to explain. Contradicting grown-ups was not allowed, but then Aunt Lavender had always considered Tavy a wilful child. 'Octavia is strong-willed and stubborn', she had written on Tavy's 'Character'. Everyone was given a 'Character' when they left Saint Agatha's. Tavy had read hers anxiously, wondering if it would deter a future employer. But Mrs. Paradine, her first Mistress, had scarcely bothered to look at it when she had engaged Tavy as a scullery maid.

"You are very small," she had remarked critically. "How old are you?"

"I'll be fifteen next month, ma'am," Tavy had said, "and I'm ever so strong."

Mrs. Paradine had laughed. "Splendid. I'm sure Cook will be delighted."

But Tavy had found that Cook was not easy to please, nor was Lutterworth, the butler. From the start, they had

4

agreed that Tavy was not only stubborn but also impertinent and troublesome.

"Needs taking down a peg," Cook had announced, clicking her tongue.

"Quite so," Lutterworth had agreed, and together they had set about it.

They were not unkind. It was for Tavy's own good. After all, Dora Spinks, the parlour maid, was no trouble. She did as she was told, without arguing. In Tavy's opinion, Dora Spinks was a ninny. It was only Tom Grundy, the footman, who made her life at 22 Cadogan Square bearable. Grundy was a clown and a tease and he made Tavy laugh. What's more, if it had not been for Grundy, she might still have been there now because she would have forgotten all about the poster.

She had seen it one wet Thursday afternoon while she was waiting at the bus stop. Cook had sent her to buy a pound of flour, with strict instructions to hurry back because Madam had ordered scones for tea. Tavy had held the basket under her cape while she waited for the horse bus, but the rain had splashed up round her legs every time a carriage rattled past and, dodging the umbrellas, she had retreated into a doorway.

"Spare a copper, girlie." The tattered old man standing beside her had thrust out his cap. "Kind girlie, just a copper or two."

Tavy had turned away. There were beggars everywhere, crippled, pitiful. But she only had her twopenny fare. She had stared fixedly at the poster behind her. It sagged from the wall, the writing blurred with damp. One word stood out: 'AUSTRALIA'. Where was that? Underneath was written: 'The Committee for Immigration. Single women desirous of bettering their condition by emigrating to the highly prosperous and healthy colony of Australia are offered passage on payment of Five Pounds in the Splendid Teak Built Ship, *Henrietta*, of 513 tons register which will sail from the Port of London on the fifth day of June 1849 direct for Sydney.' Something had nudged against Tavy's basket. As she swung round, the old beggar shrank back into his corner, huddled in his coat. At the same moment, there was a bustle on the pavement as the bus drew in to the stop.

It had been two days later that she had remembered the poster. There had been a dinner party upstairs, with a great many dirty dishes. She was at the sink when she had heard Grundy say, "That fellow on Madam's left, appetite like a horse, he had. Thought he'd never finish."

"I'll wager Australia will suit him admirably then," Lutterworth had remarked.

"Australia?" Tavy had echoed from the scullery. "Why's that, Mr. Lutterworth?"

"A large country for large men with large appetites," Mr. Lutterworth had pronounced with ponderous wit.

"How d'you know? Have you been there?"

"No need to be impertinent, miss."

There was a snort from Grundy. Dora sniggered.

"But I wasn't being. I mean, you've been to France. You're always telling us."

"Australia happens to be on the other side of the world," Lutterworth had informed Tavy in a withering voice.

All the same, when the dishes were finished and they were drinking tea in the servants' dining room, Tavy had persisted. "What's it like then, Australia I mean?"

"Well," Grundy had said, tilting back his chair and grinning at her, "if you dig a hole and go on deep enough, you'll get there. It's all upside down, o'course. Folks walking about on their heads with their legs in the air."

"Lawks!" Dora had gaped at him, and Cook had sniffed. She was given to sniffing.

"Go on with you, Tom Grundy," Tavy had said. "What's it really like?"

"That fella upstairs thought it was jolly enough, but it sounds a bit lonely to my way of thinking. Not many people, miles and miles of land where no white man's ever been, forests, mountains, rivers, great big parrots flying about wild, lots of them kangaroos like we saw in the Zoo and . . ."

"And savages," Cook had added caustically. "Heathen savages what eats their babies."

"Nice and tender," Grundy had said with a wink at Tavy, causing Dora to shudder and Lutterworth, who considered himself an authority, to point out that many of our undesirable criminals had been transported to Australia.

"Sounds a dreadful place," Cook had said.

But the young man upstairs didn't think so, for Grundy had heard him say that he could not wait to return. He missed the Australian sunshine. It didn't rain much and there was no fog. "No fog!" Tavy had marvelled. So you could see the sky, patterned with clouds or bright with stars. In London the sky was veiled in fog.

That night, Tavy had stood on her bed, leaning out of the small attic window. The rain had cleared, a misty moon glowed over the rooftops and high above was one star, faint and distant, hundreds, no thousands of miles away. It made London seem small and insignificant. Yet Tavy had never been anywhere else. She envied the man who had been to Australia, had the chance to go back ... Well, according to the poster she had seen at the bus stop, if you were a single woman with five pounds you could go there too. She had no relations at all and there were five gold sovereigns in her little leather purse, so ... The very thought of it was so overpowering that she had sat down suddenly on her bed, clasping her head in her hands. It was madness, of course, a fantastic sort of dream, but somehow she could not put it out of her mind.

She had gone on pestering Grundy to tell her about Australia, although he had already related all he had heard several times over.

"Thinking of turning into a topsy-turvy kangaroo, are you?" he had teased. "Then you'd better practise this." And he had stood on his head against the pantry wall. Tavy had tried it too until a pile of plates had crashed to the floor. There had been heavy footsteps from outside, the door had swung open and there was Lutterworth with an expression of doom. Standing amidst the broken china, it had been no

7

use explaining that it was an accident, worse when Tavy had mentioned that Grundy had been helping her learn to stand on her head. He was given a week's notice and Tavy was sent to the Mistress to apologise.

Tavy had missed Grundy. Life at Cadogan Square was no fun without his joking and larking about. She had taken refuge in her dreams about Australia, picturing the huge sun-drenched land, the mountains, forests and strange bright birds, letting the images drift through her head as she swept and scrubbed and polished.

On her next day off, she had walked back to the poster, just to look at it, she had told herself, just to make sure she had not imagined the whole thing, not because she was really considering the idea. No, she just wanted to look. She had stood for a long time in front of the poster, reading it carefully because some of the words were unknown to her. At the bottom, in very small print, was written 'Females wishing to apply should present themselves with testament of good character to Jacob Pickering, Agent to the Committee, at 26 Farthing Lane, Cornhill, London'. A testament of good character; what hope was there that Mrs. Paradine would write her a good one after her behaviour with Grundy? She had sighed resignedly, turned away and walked on down the street. So that was that. Well, she hadn't actually intended to apply, had she? It would be ever so unwise, not, in Aunt Lavender's words, a sensible way to behave. But then, at the thought of Aunt Lavender, she had stopped abruptly in the middle of the pavement, oblivious of the curious glances of passers-by. The 'Character' Aunt Lavender had given her was safely tucked away in her top drawer. She could show that to Mr. Jacob Pickering. It was not perfect; she was 'strong-willed and stubborn' but at least she was 'honest and dependable' as well, so perhaps it would pass. At any rate it was worth a try. And she had turned round and run back to have another look at the poster.

From then on, Tavy had decided to go. Apart from the adventure, the longing for freedom and space, it had been a challenge. It would not be easy, it would take courage to go so far to a completely unknown place, but that had made her all the more determined. She had kept the thought of Australia like a warm bubble of excitement inside her, a secret bubble, for, although she longed to talk about it, she had known that the other servants would consider her mad. Of course there were moments when she had wondered if she was, when the whole idea frightened her and she longed for someone like Grundy to give her support.

She had felt like that as she waited on the steps of 26 Farthing Lane. A clerk had ushered her into the office of Mr. Jacob Pickering, a grey, spindly man with a brittle voice.

"So you wish to emigrate to Australia?" he had said, peering at Tavy over his half-moon spectacles, when he had finished studying her 'Character'.

"Yes, sir."

"You are exceedingly small. Are you healthy?"

"Oh yes, sir."

"A robust constitution is essential," he had told her sternly. "The Colonies are no place for a weakling."

"I'm not a weakling," Tavy had protested indignantly, her courage fully restored. No one had ever called her a weakling before. She had lifted her chin and looked Mr. Jacob Pickering straight in the eye.

"I'm used to hard work sir. We all had to help at Saint Agatha's, even the littlest ones, cooking, scrubbing, washing the sheets. It wasn't no soft life, sir, I can tell you. And I'm a scullery maid now. Maybe you think working in Cadogan Square sounds grand, sir, but if you knew Cook and Mr. Lutterworth . . ."

"Yes, yes, quite so." Mr. Jacob Pickering had raised a hand. He had no time to waste listening to aspiring emigrants' life stories. Tavy had clearly demonstrated her eagerness, her testament appeared to be in order. Therefore if she would sign her name — she had written 'Octavia Mary Finch' with great care, pressing the quill so hard that ink splattered over the page — the charge, payable on application, was five pounds. He had watched impatiently as Tavy had pulled open her little leather purse and counted out five gold sovereigns. For a moment, seeing them lie gleaming on the desk, Tavy had been filled with doubt. It was all the money her father had left her. Was it right to spend it like this? Was she really sure? But then Mr. Jacob Pickering's long bony fingers had gathered them up — and that had been that. Her ticket would be available at the office of the Ocean and Colonial Shipping Company in Charing Cross Road a week before embarkation; a handshake, a frosty smile, a good afternoon, and Tavy had found herself outside on the pavement. It had been drizzling, people with umbrellas had jostled into her, a passing cart had sprayed her with mud and suddenly she had thought of sunshine, of clear blue skies and open land. Australia! She really was going to Australia. In only five weeks, she would sail away, over the seas and a great way off. There was a song that went like that. And, with excitement tingling right down to her toes, she had skip-hopped along the street singing aloud ". . . over the sea and a great way off, the wind will blow my topknot off."

She had had to give a month's notice. "Well, it's not that I'm unhappy, ma'am, not really. But you see, I've never been out of London in all my life and . . ."

"Yes, I see, Spinks."

"I'm Finch, ma'am."

"Finch, of course." The Mistress, adjusting her ringlets in the looking glass, had seemed unconcerned.

And then the news had reached the servants' hall. Lutterworth had maintained a frosty silence. Cook had been sure that Tavy would regret it; didn't know when she was well off, that was her trouble, not like Dora. Dora had looked smug. "What are you going to do then, Tavy?" she had asked.

"Oh, something will turn up," Tavy had assured her airily. She had left Cadogan Square with no regrets. Then, with four days until the ship sailed, she had gone back to Saint Agatha's.

"Octavia, dear child! How delightful to see you!" Aunt Lavender had clasped her to her generous bosom. "But

Australia — so far and you such a scrap. Why there, my pet?"

It had been no use trying to explain. Aunt Lavender had not been able to understand. But although, even for so short a time, Tavy had felt caged by the old routine, it had been very hard to say goodbye.

It had taken her a long time to find her way to the docks and, standing on the quay with the masts of the *Henrietta* towering above her, she had felt lonely and isolated. But, watching the knots of people round her, clustered together, arms entwined, she had been glad there was nobody to see her off.

There had been the final farewells, the clasping, weeping, the last lingering touch and then Tavy had been swept into the surging crowd, struggling over the gangway with her heavy bag. Once on board, she had stood at the deck rail looking down at the upturned faces, the fluttering handkerchiefs, the rubbish bobbing in the dirty river. There had been shouts from the quayside, the whip of ropes being hauled aboard, a sudden urgency from the passengers, waving, calling "Goodbye, goodbye", as slowly the *Henrietta* had begun to move. Gradually the brown water had widened, patterned with swirls of yellow scum, the faces on the quay had blurred together and wharves and boatyards had come into view. "Make all plain sail." The cry had been echoed along the ship. There had been sailors up the rigging, quick, sure-footed. And then, with a great beating and flapping like hundreds of sheets hung out to dry, the sails were unfurled. They had begun to move faster, driven by the wind, leaving the paddle tugs far behind. Tavy had looked up at the billowing sails, at the screeching gulls wheeling overhead and she had felt her heart lift. They were on their way. The voyage had begun.

Chapter Two

It was very quiet, very still. Tavy stared up at the lanterns hanging from the deckhead. They had been swinging to and fro with the movement of the ship. Now they were barely stirring. She must have dozed off. Was it daylight yet? Without portholes it was impossible to tell.

She slid from her berth, landing with a soft thump beside Annie Button, snoring steadily flat on her back. Looking round, she noticed that most people were still asleep. Carrying her boots, Tavy tiptoed towards the steps, clambered up, pushed open the hatch and there she was, out on deck.

It was not yet day. The sky glowed strangely in the half light, pale and translucent like Mrs. Paradine's pearls. The *Henrietta* was scudding gently towards a narrow gap between two headlands. There was a flash, a path of brightness on the metallic sea. The Macquarie Lighthouse? Yes, Tavy could see it now, rising above the South Head, and below there were buildings nestling along the lower slopes. The other headland was steep, jutting sharply down to the water's edge, deep in shadow. She would have to wait for the sun to rise before she could see more. The deck was almost deserted; only a few figures stood huddled over the deck rail, staring towards the land. Tavy pulled her shawl tightly round her shoulders. After weeks of sailing through the tropics, where the sun beat down like fire, she had almost forgotten what it felt like to be cold. Her hiding place would be sheltered from the wind. Near the main mast, she climbed on a ledge and tucked herself in beside one of the boats. She had spent countless hours there during the journey, reading — she soon knew both *The Forbidden Promise* and *Rose of the Glen* by heart — or dreaming about Australia as she gazed at the sea and the changing sky. Sometimes, during the worst of the heat, she had stayed there all night. It was cramped and uncomfortable not being able to stretch out and she hadn't slept much, but anything was better than the stifling heat of the lower deck.

"Where d'you disappear to?" Annie Button had asked. "You haven't gone after that sailor of yours, have you?"

Tavy had been indignant. "The very idea!" Duggan was just a friend. And she had decided not to tell Annie about her hiding place. There was not room for two there anyway. Annie was big and noisy. She would have chattered all the time and they would have been discovered.

The darkness was fading now. More passengers had come on deck, pacing up and down to keep themselves warm. She caught sight of Duggan walking past with a bucket and, jumping down, ran after him.

"Duggan." She touched his arm. He looked round.

"Tavy! You still up here?"

"I wanted to see if we were there yet. Are we?"

"At Sydney?"

"Yes."

"Not long now. Have to wait for the wind. Should freshen around midday."

"Midday! That's not for hours."

Duggan shook his head at her. "See here, lass. You've been aboard for fifteen weeks or so now. A few more hours isn't going to make much difference, is it?"

Tavy frowned. "It's just that I'm longing and longing to see what it's like."

Duggan shrugged. "Well, it's not paradise, not Sydney at any rate. I can promise you that."

For a moment, Tavy watched him walk on along the deck. Then she called after him. "Duggan?"

He turned his head. "What is it now?"

"Where is it?"

"Where's what?"

"Sydney."

He grinned. "You see that gap between Sydney Heads? The harbour's through there. We should be anchored in Sydney Cove by tonight. Then you'll see it all right."

Tonight. There was all day to get through and nothing to do except pack her bag, and that wouldn't take long. She had spent over a hundred days on board doing nothing at all, but now that Australia was actually in sight, her patience had suddenly run out. It had been different during the voyage. They had called into port several times. Only the first class passengers had been allowed ashore but, although there were grumbles on the lower deck, Tavy had not cared. She had felt too weak after the long bout of seasickness. At Capetown, they had taken on supplies of fruit — bananas, grapes, mandarins and oranges. They were fresh and delicious after the weeks of dried meat and rice. Everyone had feasted before they went bad, but Tavy's stomach had rebelled again.

"You'll fade away, lass," Duggan had said, finding her on deck at dinner time.

"I'm ever so strong," Tavy had assured him, though she felt as limp as a rag. Her clothes hung on her and, catching sight of herself in the washroom mirror, she had been surprised at her thin cheeks. Not that she was the only seasick passenger. There were many who seldom left their berths. Indeed there had been times when the *Henrietta* had seemed to stand on end, when boxes, cooking pots, bedding, plates, anything that was not fastened down had been flung across the lower deck, when Tavy had expected them all to be drowned. She felt so ill that she almost wished for it to happen. But Duggan had told her that it had been an easy voyage. He could remember one trip to Sydney when twenty-two people had been buried at sea after an outbreak of dysentery. Another time there had been an epidemic of measles.

14

"Spread like fire, it did, and the ship lay at anchor for three weeks' quarantine before anyone was allowed ashore."

"I'd swim if that happened," Tavy had said, although she didn't know how.

As Duggan had predicted, around midday the sky cleared and a fresh wind sprang up, filling the sails. By now everyone had come on deck. Tavy who, apart from a brief dash below to pack her belongings, had been waiting there since before dawn, was squeezed against the deck rail up in the bows when at last the *Henrietta* swung sharply to the south and sailed through the Heads.

"Oh!" The crowd on deck breathed a sigh of wonder. For there it was. Sydney harbour spread before them in the sunshine. Across the glistening water were countless bays, sheltered coves, wide sandy beaches, narrow inlets tucked between rocky promontories. It was suddenly calm; the wind had dropped and the *Henrietta*, her topsails furled, drifted lazily ahead to join the many other ships in the harbour. Over to the south through the throng of tall-masted vessels lying at anchor, Tavy could see the town. In the distance, it looked like a child's picture, its many-coloured roofs clustered along the shore and the slopes of the hill behind. Towards the North Head, the land was thickly wooded with only small settlements of buildings beside the water.

"What a sight!"

"Look at that!"

"Oh, it's beautiful!" Excited voices called all round Tavy.

"Them trees," said Annie Button who was just behind her. "There's ever such big woods over there. Can you see, Tavy?"

Tavy nodded. Oh yes, she could see all right; every part of her was concentrated on taking in the glory of this first real look at Australia. Even from the ship there was a feeling of size — those forests to the north, the hills behind the town, rolling away into the distance. And the sky; was it

15

because it no longer merged into the endless sea that it seemed different, more positive, almost powerful, a great arc of blue above the land?

The *Henrietta* dropped her anchor about half a mile from the shore but, to Tavy's great disappointment, nobody left the ship that day. She had waited, dressed in her bonnet and shawl, her bag beside her, till it grew dark.

"Come on, Tavy," Annie Button had urged. "They're having a bit of a party and a sing-song down below. You don't want to miss the fun."

"I'm all right up here," Tavy had told her stubbornly.

It was only Duggan who had eventually convinced her that there'd be no going ashore till the next day. "The Customs Inspector's not been out to clear us yet, so it's not a penn'orth of use you hanging about up here, girl. Down you go and get your beauty sleep."

It was the middle of the morning before a dinghy full of first class passengers was rowed in to the quay. Tavy went in search of Duggan. "When will it be our turn?"

Duggan was hauling boxes up from the hold, his face streaming with sweat, his temper short. "Can't wait to see the back of me, is that it?"

"No, Duggan, no. I didn't mean . . ."

But he had heaved a massive crate on to his shoulder and was staggering over to the side. Tavy sighed. She was weary with waiting. But then so was everybody else. The excitement of entering the harbour had given way to listless exhaustion after the long strain of the voyage. People hung about on deck with their bags and bundles, babies whined and children ran about, getting in the way. At last, by persistently worming her way through the confused straggle, Tavy managed to get herself to the top of the embarkation ladder. A sailor took her bag and steadied the ropes as she climbed down. Suddenly she stopped. Duggan! She hated to leave without seeing him again. She looked up, searching for him. "Come on, missie," urged the sailor.

"Duggan!" shouted Tavy. There he was, near the foremast, securing the halyards.

He glanced round then, noticing her, he smiled and waved. "Good luck, lass."

"Goodbye, Duggan, goodbye." She waved vigorously, shaking the ladder.

"Steady!" warned the sailor and the coxswain scowled as she stepped into the dinghy.

"I'm sorry, sir," Tavy said to him, though she was not really sorry. Duggan had been a good friend all through the long voyage, so it had been most important to say goodbye to him.

"Wake up, child. It's time you raised yourself." Tavy opened her eyes and looked up into a ruddy face surrounded by straggly hair escaping from a mob-cap. Where was she?

"The rest of 'em's gone down to the employment office," said the woman. "You'd best get along there too or you'll miss your chance of a job." She twitched back the curtains. Sun streamed through the small window. Tavy sat up and rubbed her eyes. She was in the corner of a low-ceilinged room with a rough wooden floor. The row of beds beside hers was empty, though the blankets were rumpled and garments lay scattered around. Now she remembered. This was the female immigrants' hostel and the woman who had just shuffled out was Mrs. Trumper, the Matron. She had come here with Annie Button yesterday when, after another long wait, they had been allowed to leave the Registration Office on the quayside. Carrying their bags, they had climbed the hill towards the town along unpaved streets lined with single-storey cottages. Laden waggons pulled by teams of bullocks had trundled slowly past them, lurching over the muddy ruts; skinny brown dogs roamed about, sniffing at the piles of manure and rubbish which lay scattered everywhere.

Annie Button had pulled a face. "Ugh! It's dreadfully dirty!"

"But the sky's lovely and blue," Tavy had said, looking

17

up. "And we are on dry land." Her land of promise. Australia. She wasn't going to hear a word of criticism about it, although privately she had to admit that this part of Sydney was . . . well, not quite as she had expected, certainly not as idyllic as it had appeared in the distance. Later, leaving Annie Button to gossip with the others at the hostel, she had slipped out alone to explore.

It was already dark, but a damp mist was rising from the harbour, hiding the stars. The only light came through the cottage windows so that Tavy had had to pick her way carefully to avoid the rubbish. She had been surprised that there were so many people about, strolling along, stopping to chat or sitting outside their houses, apparently oblivious of the stench and the prowling dogs. Some had called to her — "Evening, girlie", "Nice night for a stroll" or "How are you, missie?". But she had hurried past, pretending not to notice.

At the end of one street, lanterns hung outside a tall building on the corner, throwing a pool of light on the ground. Tavy had crossed over, keeping in the shadows, for she had seen the sign The Sailor's Return and she knew that in London it was best to avoid taverns after dark. Coming nearer, she had heard shouting and singing from inside, a strong smell of liquor wafted through the doors as men, and women too, pushed their way in, and she had seen with horror that there were bodies sprawled in the mud outside. She had run down the hill towards the harbour, then stopped. It would surely be better further away from the docks. Around the next corner, she had come to a steep flight of steps. Across the top was a wider street, with terraced houses two storeys high along both sides. She had turned left and walked on. It had been cleaner, there were trees here and there and pale petals of blossom lay on the ground. But further along, she had seen another tavern and had run back the way she had come. It was then that she had noticed footsteps behind her; they had seemed to come closer and, as she had increased her speed, she had heard a shout. With her heart pounding in her ears, she had dived down an alleyway between the houses. In the total darkness, something small had scuttled from under her feet and she had stopped, gasping with fear, then, stumbling on over the rough ground, she had emerged into an open square. There were people, horse-drawn carts, small shops still open, another tavern. Lanterns swung in the wind so that the whole scene seemed to sway from side to side and, for a moment, Tavy had felt herself back on board ship. As she had stood catching her breath, something had caught at her dress. She had cried out in alarm, wrenching herself away. Her dress had ripped, but she had fled without looking round, along street after street, her panic growing as she had realised she was completely lost. For hours it seemed, she had struggled on, sobbing aloud with fear and desolation. Would it all be like this, frightening and wicked and dirty? Oh, why had she come? She had longed for Aunt Lavender, for Grundy, for Duggan. "Not paradise," he had said. Yes, now she knew. She could hardly remember reaching the hostel again at last, only the relief of suddenly recognising the heavy wooden door, of trying the handle and finding it unlocked. Then groping her way up the narrow stairs and falling onto her bed overwhelmed with exhaustion.

"I've kept you some breakfast," said Mrs. Trumper, when Tavy went down to the kitchen. She looked Tavy up and down. "You look as if you could do with it too," she added.

Tavy smoothed her crumpled dress. She had changed from the torn one into another from her bag, but it seemed to be several sizes too big for her. Mrs. Trumper placed a bowl of porridge in front of her and Tavy ate gratefully. She kept her head down, fearing that Mrs. Trumper would ask her why she had missed supper last night and stayed out so late. But Mrs. Trumper hummed tunelessly to herself as she fetched a pitcher of milk, a jar of jam, a large flat loaf and placed them on the table in front of Tavy

"You put plenty of jam on the damper," she ordered. "Fatten yourself up a bit."

The 'damper' tasted like home-made scones and the milk

was fresh and creamy. When Tavy had finished, she glanced up to find Mrs. Trumper smiling at her approvingly. Shafts of sunlight streamed through the windows , outside she could see a bush of crimson flowers against a clear sky and she wondered whether perhaps Australia might not be so disappointing after all.

"Next."

Tavy jumped up. The man behind the desk was looking directly at her. There was, in fact, no one else waiting. Tavy was the last. For the past three hours, she had been sitting on a hard wooden bench in the Female Employment Office while one by one the other emigrants from the *Henrietta* applied for vacancies. The employment officer, a rotund, bearded man, took her name, age — raising his eyebrows when she said she was fifteen — and read through her testimonial.

"Well, there's not much left for domestics," he said running his finger down the page of the ledger, "not in Sydney, at any rate."

"Oh, no!" Tavy said quickly. "Not Sydney." The man glanced up, surprised at the urgency in her voice. "I mean, well sir, I've always lived in London and I'd like a change. The country would be different, if you take my meaning, sir, and . . ."

"It would be different all right," said the employment officer bluntly. "You might find it rather too different. Most girls coming out on their own would rather stay in the town. Life in the bush can be lonely and hard. You need a strong constitution."

"I know about that, sir," Tavy assured him. "The colonies are no place for a weakling." Mr. Jacob Pickering had told her that. "And I'm not, sir, not a weakling, I mean. I know I'm small," she went on, before he could say it for her, "but I'm ever so strong and besides," she added with sudden inspiration, "the country air might make me grow."

The employment officer looked at her doubtfully. "You

20

appear," he said, "to be very determined."

"I am," Tavy said.

She waited while he consulted his ledger. " 'Experienced cook required, two days' travel from Gunderra,' " he read out. "Are you an experienced cook, Miss Finch?"

"I can peel the vegetables," Tavy said, "and I always washed up and . . ."

The employment officer shook his head. " 'Governess over eighteen years of age'— no, that won't suit. Let me see. 'Responsible girl to care for two young children and a baby. Experience essential.' "

"I could do that," Tavy said eagerly. "I used to help with the juniors when I was in the Orphanage and . . ."

"Babies?" inquired the employment officer.

"Well, not babies. They lived in a separate nursery. But the juniors were dear little souls, sir. I'm ever so experienced with them, and I'd love to care for a baby."

Again the employment officer shook his head and his finger moved slowly down the list. "There is one here," he said. Tavy held her breath. " 'Wanted: girl for general household duties'. That sounds possible."

Tavy nodded. "When shall I start?"

"You'll have to get there first, young lady. It's on a property called Tallangatta, belongs to a Mr. Campion, six miles beyond Burrawong Creek. That's a fair way." He unfolded a map and spread it out on the desk. "Burrawong Creek," he muttered, frowning at the map. "Mmm, it's right out beyond Gunderra township. There's nothing much else around there."

"I'll be happy with that, sir," Tavy said. "I don't like crowds."

The employment officer snorted. "There'll be no crowds, not unless you are reckoning on sheep. It'll be getting yourself there will be the trouble. There'll be a coach going to Gunderra, but from there you'll just have to wait for someone going west who will give you a ride."

"That'll be quite all right, thank you sir," said Tavy. "But," she paused a moment, looking at him anxiously,

"I've not much money left for my fare. You see, I saved four and threepence from my wages but the hostel costs ninepence a day and . . ."

"Your fare is paid by your employer. That is the usual arrangement," he told her, glancing at the ledger. "Hmm, yes. 'Wages seventeen and sixpence a month, coach fare five shillings." He took a metal box from the drawer of his desk, unlocked it and counted out the coins. "The coach for Gunderra leaves tomorrow," he said, writing on a slip of paper. He handed it to her with the money. Then, closing his ledger with a purposeful thump, he put away his metal box, rose and fetched his hat. He had finished for the day.

Tavy put the coins in her purse. Then she read the slip of paper. 'Campion, Tallangatta, Burrawong Creek', signed E.B. Rudge, Employment Officer. She stared at it, entranced. Tallangatta, Burrawong Creek. The words were like music, exciting and strange. She looked up, beaming, to thank Mr. Rudge, but he had disappeared through a door at the back.

"Sounds like the back end of nowhere to me," said Annie Button, when Tavy told her where she was going. She had been engaged as a cook to a prosperous wool merchant's family at the top of Sydney Town. It was proper and respectable up there, with great big houses and gardens full of flowers. There were even palm trees like they had seen in Africa. She'd have a half day off every week, and the wages . . . ! She'd be rich in no time. Then she'd find herself a man. He'd be tall and handsome, they'd have three lovely babies. She smiled dreamily, thinking of her future.

"I'll be a fine lady with a home of my own," she said. "And you'll come and visit me, won't you, Tavy?"

Tavy promised that one day she would come back to Sydney and find Annie Button again, and she stood in the doorway waving goodbye as Annie set off, with her bundles and bags, to her grand new position at the top of the town.

22

Chapter Three

Tavy could not move. She sat squashed between the side of the coach and a large woman with a bundle on her lap. She had tried wriggling into a more comfortable position, but the woman was as firm as an upholstered couch. All the same, for the first time in her life Tavy was glad to be small because otherwise she would not have been on this coach at all. It had left that morning from Argyle Place, a steep climb up the hill from the hostel.

"You'd best be there early," Mrs. Trumper had advised. "That Gunderra coach is always full."

But when, after a hurried breakfast, Tavy had come to say goodbye, she had insisted that Tavy take a picnic for the journey. It was no use protesting that the coach might leave without her. Mrs. Trumper was adamant. Two days — at least two days — on the road without food. Nonsense! Tavy was already far too skinny. And she had been forced to wait while Mrs. Trumper buttered slices of damper, packing them with cheese and apples in a folded napkin. By the time Tavy had reached Argyle Place, the coach was full. The driver, a brawny man in a wide-brimmed hat, had been adjusting the harness on the front pair of horses.

"No room," he had said briefly, without looking at Tavy.

"Oh please, sir. I must get to Gunderra," she had begged. "I haven't got much luggage and I won't take up a lot of space."

"See here, miss, I've got too much weight on board as it

is." Then, turning to look at her, he had paused. "Littl'un, eh? Well, I don't know as how I should but your size won't make much difference. Give me that bag and hop in quick."

"Oh, thank you, sir," Tavy had beamed at him before she had scrambled up the steps and squeezed into the back seat.

The three rows of passengers, many from the *Henrietta*, sat closely jammed together, swaying from side to side as the coach lurched and jolted over the rutted roads. After a few remarks about it being a rough ride and there not being much risk of dozing off, there was little conversation. By craning her neck, Tavy could just see through the window. She caught sight of shingled roofs, an upper balcony, then trees, grey-green leaves stirring in the wind, a flicker of birds' wings, a glimpse of sky. It was tantalising not to be able to see more. She tapped her toes on the floor of the coach and wondered how soon they would stop.

At last, after several hours — or so it seemed — they began to slow down. They were climbing gradually over bumpy ground. Then they stopped, the door swung open.

"All out," shouted the driver. "You'll have to walk."

Instantly Tavy was down the steps. She stood gazing round her, entranced. For the first time in her life she was in the country, the real country, not a park like Kensington Gardens with neat lawns and flower beds. There were trees everywhere; tall graceful trees with great strips of bark peeling from their silvery trunks, dark green bushes with tiny white flowers and straggly tufts of grass as high as her waist. She sniffed the air. It smelled fragrant and faintly aromatic, like the eucalyptus Aunt Lavender had used to treat stuffy noses. She wandered away, ignoring the confusion as the rest of the passengers climbed out of the coach and the men put their shoulders to the rear, pushing while the horses strained to pull it up the muddy slope. Tavy followed slowly, hanging back when they reached the top, unwilling to climb inside again. When the driver asked the men to walk for a few miles until the going was easier, she offered to as well.

"Not you, missie," the driver said. "Too easy to get lost in these gum trees if you lag behind. There'll be snakes about now, dingoes too. You'd best ride. Sit up here alongside me on the box, if you like."

Perched beside the driver, Tavy felt like the Queen driving through London above the crowds, except that there were no city streets, only a rough track between the trees, no cheering crowds, only the birds calling overhead. Here and there she noticed smaller trees with vivid yellow blossom. She reached out and picked a sprig as they passed. It was soft and fluffy and the pollen made her sneeze.

"That's wattle," the driver told her. "It's late this spring. We've had so much rain."

Spring? Tavy was amazed. This was September. Then she remembered that this was the other side of the world. Here the seasons were upside down. But no English spring was ever so warm. She leaned back, letting the sun warm her face, watching it patterning the horses' sweaty backs as it filtered through the leaves above her. Big black and white birds flew out of the trees.

"Them's maggies," said the driver. "Australian ones. Not like your British kind, but they're magpies to us."

There were small birds too, the size of sparrows but bright-coloured, some with long tails, that darted in and out of the branches before Tavy could catch more than a glimpse of them. And suddenly she spotted a flash of scarlet and blue.

"What's that?" she pointed excitedly. "Up there."

The driver tipped back the brim of his hat. "Parrot," he said. "Dozens of 'em about."

"It's beautiful," Tavy exclaimed. "Look, there it goes". She had never seen a parrot before. Cook had kept a canary in a cage. 'Sweetie' was pale yellow and twittered listlessly. This bird was huge, with a strident voice and powerful wings that beat the air like the *Henrietta's* sails.

"Proper curse, them parrots," the driver told her. "Scare the horses if they fly too close. Kangaroos is worst though. They come bounding out of the bush with no warning. Drives the horses wild."

Alarming though it sounded, Tavy longed to see a kangaroo. She had seen one in the Zoo when Grundy had taken her, but it had been a sickly moth-eaten creature. When they reached open country, she scanned the bush for brown animals leaping along. Several times, something seemed to move amongst the scattered gum trees, but she could not be sure and she didn't like to mention it to the driver.

For the rest of the day the landscape was the same: rolling plains stretching away for miles and miles and over it all the vast, clear sky with the sun travelling slowly towards the distant line of hills. But it wasn't monotonous, not for Tavy. She sat straight and alert on the box, revelling in the freedom and space, the fresh warm air and the creak of the wheels as they trundled along the bumpy track. It was lovely, lovely. Her heart was singing. Yes, now she was really glad she had come.

Every so often they crossed a creek, plunging down the bank and slowly churning their way through the swirling brown water. Once they came to a river, spanned by a narrow wooden bridge. Again all the passengers had to get out while the driver led the horses across. Tavy watched anxiously, for the bridge looked far too rickety for the massive carriage with its roof piled with baggage. But as soon as it was safely on the far bank, she ran over quickly to reclaim her place on the box before the driver offered it to anyone else.

At last, when the sun was almost touching the hills and the horizon was tinged with pink, they turned off the track and stopped near a shallow creek.

"We'll spend the night here," the driver said, laying down his whip. "But where will we sleep?" Tavy asked.

"Anywhere you like, miss," he grinned at her. "Inside, outside, underneath."

Tavy knew at once which she would choose. She had never slept out of doors before. She set off to find a sheltered place, away from the coach, where she could lie in the grass and watch the stars. But as soon as the sun went down — a great crimson ball staining the sky — the air grew cold.

Some of the passengers from the *Henrietta* stood huddled together shivering, bewildered by the strangeness of it all. But not Tavy. Even after the long day's ride, she felt exhilarated by the sense of space all round her. She helped to collect sticks for the fire and watched two of the women brew tea. 'Billy tea' they called it and, though Tavy considered boiling it in a tin pail an odd way to make it, she accepted a cup gladly. It was hot and sweet and she was thirsty. The warmth of the fire made her drowsy. There was a chilly wind rushing through the trees. Perhaps she'd change her mind about sleeping on her own. There was a feeling of easy companionship; food was shared, one man passed round a bottle of rum, another fetched his fiddle and played a tune. Tavy stared at the sky and it seemed to her that the sad thin music came from the stars, as if they were singing far away. It was a different song on this side of the world because here the stars were upside down.

Tavy stood just inside the Gunderra Central Hotel, her bag beside her. The smoky, low-ceilinged room was full of people, most of them men — enormous men they seemed to Tavy — in broad-brimmed hats and leather trousers, drinking tankards of ale, shouting and bellowing with laughter. She had hesitated before venturing inside, for the noise and fumes of alcohol wafting through the door reminded her of the taverns in Sydney. "You try in the hotel," the coach driver had advised her when she had asked him how to get to Burrawong Creek. "There's sure to be someone in there who'll know". It would have helped if there were other passengers from the coach going that way. Tavy had asked them all, but no one had even heard of it.

After three nights on the road, they had all become friends, shaking hands warmly and waving goodbye each time they stopped to let somebody get off. Though there was plenty of room inside the coach Tavy had refused to leave her place on the box. "I like it here," she had told the driver firmly, and through four days she had sat beside him watching the vast country all round her, the scrubby bush, forests of gum trees, the endless miles of open plain. It had been dusk when the coach had trundled into Gunderra. They had seen it in the distance, a small settlement planted in a dip. There was little but the one main street, a muddy thoroughfare lined with squat, shabby cottages on either side. Cows and goats grazed on the grass between them, hens scratched in the mud and, ahead of the coach, a flock of sheep straggled behind a bullock dray piled high with bundles. As they went by, people had run out of their houses to wave, barefoot children and barking dogs had chased them all the way down the street until they stopped in front of the hotel. Tavy had waited by the coach while the driver had unloaded the baggage, watching the other passengers climb out. She had envied some of the women who had come out to join their husbands, looking round anxiously, then with cries of happiness rushing forward to be met, embraced and led away. They had reached the end of their journey.

The other passengers had either set off for addresses in Gunderra or gone straight into the hotel. Tavy tried to see them amongst the crowd of drinkers, but they seemed to have disappeared. She looked round, wondering who to ask about getting to Burrawong Creek. That man by the door, with his back to her? As if he had read her thoughts, he turned round, saw Tavy and winked. She felt herself go pink and hung her head.

"Was you waiting for someone, little missie?" Tavy looked up. The man had come over to her and was leaning with one hand against the wall above her head. His hat was tilted back, his face gleamed with sweat. Tavy shook her head. He waved a bottle at her.

"Care for a drink?"

"No thank you, sir."

"Sir! Well, I'm blowed! 'Sir' she called me. I like that, little missie. I like that a lot."

He put back his head and guffawed with laughter. Tavy looked round desperately. How could she escape? The man was clearly dreadfully tipsy. Any moment, she was sure, he would strike her with his bottle. She picked up her carpet bag and dived under his arm.

"Watch where you're going, will you?" A stout woman with a tray glared at Tavy. "You nearly had me dropping the lot."

"I'm sorry, ma'am, but it's that man. I had to get away. I think he's . . . I'm afraid he's tipsy."

"They're all tipsy. It's always like this on a market day." The woman looked at Tavy. "What are you doing here? This is no place for a little girl on her own."

Tavy was indignant. "I'm fifteen, ma'am, and I came on the coach from Sydney and the driver told me to come in here and ask how to get to Burrawong Creek."

"Burrawong Creek?" She frowned and shook her head. "Don't know myself, but Paddy'll tell you. He's the proprietor and he just about knows everyone round these parts. You come along to the kitchen with me and we'll ask him."

Paddy, a rotund bearded Irishman, was seated at the kitchen table, eating an enormous plateful of food.

"Let's see now." He wiped the stew off his beard with the back of his hand. "Sure and I'm after thinking that's away out to the west, a fair way, mind you. But don't you worry, my lovely, we'll find someone to take you."

"Didn't that Willie Moser take up a run over there?" said a girl who was rinsing beer mugs in a low stone sink.

"Mmmm," Paddy nodded, his mouth full. But the woman with the tray thumped it down in front of him.

"I wouldn't trust that Willie Moser as far as the end of my nose," she said. "Certainly not with a scrap of a child like this."

There she goes again, Tavy thought, and she stuck out her chin and said, "I've come all the way from London on my own, ma'am, and I do know how to look after myself."

"Oh, old Will's all right," said Paddy. "Wouldn't hurt a fly when he's sober. He'll have such a sore head after tonight he won't touch another drop till next market day. Sure an' he'll take you tomorrow all right."

"Tomorrow?' Tavy looked at them anxiously.

"Bless you, child!" said Paddy, rising to his feet and hitching up his trousers. "You wouldn't be going any place tonight! Why 'tis near enough dark. You can stay here. Mary'll fix you up with a bed and bite of supper."

"Course I will," said the first woman in a motherly voice. "We're pretty full up but we can squeeze you in and no bother." She picked up Tavy's carpet bag and started towards the door, but Tavy caught her arm.

"The trouble is, ma'am, I've only got sevenpence because I had to buy some food on the way. We stopped at a store and, you see, everyone in the coach shared and . . . "

"Don't you worry, my lovely," Paddy interrupted. "You have a night on the house. It'll hardly be the ruin of us with the fortune that hooley out there's spending on their ale."

The 'hooley' went on far into the night. As Tavy lay on a low bed in the attic above the saloon, the whole building seemed to vibrate with noise. But she was warm, full of supper and far too tired to worry about Willie Moser and tomorrow. In a very few moments, the noise became part of her dreams.

It had rained the whole day — well it seemed like the whole day to Tavy though for all she knew there might still be a considerable amount of day left. Without the sun, it was impossible to tell. Her clothes were soaked through and she certainly felt as if she had been sitting in the back of Willie Moser's horse-drawn cart for at least a day, jolting over rough ground and lurching into pot holes hidden under tussocks of coarse grass. Of course it would have been less uncomfortable on the driver's seat but, after Mary's remarks the night before, nothing would have persuaded her to ask Willie Moser if she could squeeze in beside him. She had woken up early with a tight, anxious feeling in the pit of her stomach. Supposing Willie Moser turned out to be that man who had spoken to her in the saloon? She dared not think what might happen to her. Could she refuse to

30

go? But then she might not get another chance of a lift for weeks. Perhaps there would be other passengers; perhaps Mrs. Willie Moser might be with him.

There was nobody else, just her and Willie Moser but, to her great relief, he was a thin, leathery man with drooping shoulders and a long red nose — Willie 'Noser', she had thought the moment she saw him. He had merely grunted and nodded his head when Paddy had asked him to take Tavy to Burrawong Creek and, before she could add that she actually wanted to go a few miles further to Tallangatta, he had muttered something about it being time he was shifting and stumped out of the hotel. By the time Tavy had thanked Mary and Paddy, promised to come back and see them one day, accepted a packet of food for the journey and said goodbye, Willie Moser was sitting on his cart in the steady rain and she had only just had time to climb on the back before he had picked up the reins and started away.

There was little else on the back of the cart; a few sacks of some sort of grain, boxes labelled tea, rice, flour, sugar, several stone jars and some big baskets filled with a jumble of provisions. Clearly Willie Moser had stocked up at the Gunderra stores. At first, she had tried wedging herself between sacks of grain, but they kept slipping away. Then she had sat with her legs dangling over the back, but mud spattered up her skirts and she had been afraid she might fall off the end. She had tried lying down — that was hopeless — so was perching on her carpet bag because, each time the cart went over a bump, she had bounced off. In the end she had given up and just let herself be shaken and bruised on the rough boards. It would not have been so bad if the sun had been shining. Of course she knew it had to rain sometimes. The coach driver had told her it had been a wet spring, and they had been stuck in the mud several times. But though there was still that feeling of space, the countryside looked grey and monotonous. Certainly, grey skies and rain did not fit in with her dream of Australia, besides making it much harder to remain cheerful in the back of this cart. My bottom will be black and blue, she had

31

thought. She would look like one of those monkeys she had seen in the Zoo when she went with Grundy. They had been funny. Just remembering it had made her giggle.

"Eh?" Willie Moser had peered round at her, rain dripping off the brim of his soggy hat, and Tavy, who had been equally suprised at the sound of her own laughter, had said, "Oh — er, nothing sir. I just thought of something funny." She was relieved when, with a loud sniff, Willie Moser had turned round again. Otherwise he had scarcely spoken all day. His continual silence made her uneasy. She watched the horizon anxiously. The mountains were behind them now; ahead was an empty stretch of plain. There was no sign of Burrawong Creek.

The rain was easing at last, the clouds drifting apart. Then a gleam of sun broke through, low in the sky. It would soon be dusk. Willie Moser stopped the cart under a clump of gum trees, climbed down stiffly and took off his hat. His sparse grey hair clung to his head in damp wisps. He sniffed and rubbed his nose.

"Good place," he said. "Always make for this waterhole."

His voice took Tavy by surprise. "Beg pardon, sir?" she said.

"Waterhole." He waved towards a pond just beyond the trees. "Get a fire going. Cook some tucker. Dry your clothes, eh?" His face creased into a toothless grin.

Tavy did not answer. He meant to stay here for the night. She looked round at the deserted landscape, the darkening sky. She was all alone with this queer old man, miles and miles from anywhere. She stood by the cart watching him tether the horse, unpack his provisions, collect sticks and build a fire. It won't burn, Tavy thought. It must be far too damp. But perhaps it had not rained here for, when Willie Moser struck a match on the sole of his boot, the kindling caught at once, flickering, growing, flames like tongues. He took off his coat and hung it over a branch next to his soggy hat. He nodded at Tavy.

"You'll catch cold in them things. Strip 'em off." Tavy untied her bonnet, shook out her shawl and laid them close

32

to the fire. Willie Moser eyed her with his head on one side.

"The rest is wet too," he said. As if to demonstrate his meaning he unbuckled his belt and began to peel off his trousers.

Tavy turned away hastily. She was not a prude but, well, there were some things that were just not proper. Averting her eyes, she fetched her bag from the cart and carried it behind the trees, out of sight of Willie Moser. Away from the fire, it was suddenly cold. She searched in her bag for her torn dress, dry underclothes, shivering as she struggled out of her clammy garments. As she peeled off her stockings, a twig snapped close by. She glanced up. Willie Moser dodged back behind the trees. He had been watching her. He had seen her in nothing but her petticoat. Shocking that was! Nasty old man. Unseen in the darkness Tavy blushed. She wasn't going near him again, she thought as she struggled into her dress. Best keep away, stay round here. She sat down hugging her knees, her teeth chattering. She tried to ignore the chill creeping through her body, tried not to hear the crackle of the fire, the sizzle as Willie Moser cooked his supper. She concentrated on the soft murmuring of insects, a night bird calling, the chomp of the horse cropping grass. The horse must be hungry too.

Tavy had finished her food early in the day, and now the smell of Willie Moser's bacon and toast made her ache with emptiness. She twisted round, peering through the trees, crawling forward until she could see Willie Moser crouching over the fire in a tattered shirt and long baggy underpants. Talk about Saturday night at the Music Hall, she thought. What would Mr. Lutterworth have said! If she hadn't been so hungry and cold, it would have seemed funny. Willie Moser poked at the frying pan with a long stick, shook it and tipped the contents onto a tin plate. Then he filled a mug from the billy can, stirred in some sugar and took a gulp.

"Ah!" he sighed, wiping his mouth on his sleeve.

Tavy shut her eyes. Hot tea, warming you all the way down inside. And now — she opened her eyes and he was eating bacon and toast, potatoes too, and big chunks of meat, cramming it all into his mouth with his hands. It would soon be gone. Without thinking what she was doing, Tavy stood up and walked on through the trees, out into the open, towards the fire.

Willie Moser's head jerked up and he stared at her, his mouth full of food. He swallowed hurriedly.

"Tucker — want some?" He held up his mug. "Tea?"

Tavy nodded emphatically. As she watched him from the far side of the fire busily, almost guiltily, refilling the frying pan, she edged gradually closer, feeling the warmth penetrate her body. When the food was cooked, he placed the plate carefully on a flat stone near the fire and filled a mug with tea. His plate, Tavy thought, but she was too ravenous to care and it was a different mug.

"There y'are." He grinned at her. "Come on round 'ere."

Tavy hesitated, unwilling to go nearer, yet desperate for food. She skirted the fire and stopped, holding out her hand. Willie Moser sat down and patted the ground beside him.

" 'Ere."

Again Tavy paused. Then she darted forward, grabbed the plate and backed away. But her skirt was caught. She looked down to see Willie Moser holding it firmly.

"What's the matter wi' ya? Stay 'ere." His little red eyes leered at her. There was greasy food round his toothless mouth. What could she do? If she wrenched herself away, her dress, already torn, might rip right up, revealing her petticoat again. He was tugging at the hem as it was, to make her sit beside him. She gave up and knelt stiffly, her head turned away, eating quickly without tasting the food. She could feel his hot breath on the back of her neck. Then he was muttering in her ear.

"Pretty little thing, aren't ya? No call to be scared o' me."

She felt his hand on her side, creeping round her, his fingers like insects crawling, gripping . . .

She gave a startled cry, flung down the plate with a clatter and scurried away into the darkness.

For the rest of the night, Tavy had hidden behind the trees, growing stiff with cold. Every few moments, she had edged sideways to watch Willie Moser, but he had only moved once to fetch a bottle from the cart. Then he had sat beside the embers, drinking steadily, until he had lain down and started to snore. Towards dawn, Tavy had dropped into a half sleep, haunted by dreams of Willie Moser chasing her, shrieking with frenzied laughter. Waking in terror, she had found that the noise came from a long-beaked bird on a branch overhead.

Willie Moser had not spoken until they reached Burrawong Creek, a few crude cottages beside a bridge.

" 'Ere y'are," he had announced over his shoulder.

Tavy had known she would have to explain, be forced to plead to be taken further. "It's called Tallangatta, quite near here, I think." Her voice had been strained, close to tears. "So please, if it's not too much out of your way . . . you see, I've not enough money to stay here, just this." She had held out her remaining sevenpence. He had pocketed it without comment and stumped off to the store.

"Signpost six miles west – over the creek. Only property out that way," he had muttered when he returned and they had rumbled on through wooded grasslands.

Tavy had struggled to keep awake, but the movement of the cart had proved too much. She had woken to find they were standing in a clearing.

"That's it," Willie Moser had said, jerking his head towards a small log hut thatched with strips of bark. He had heaved down her bag, touched his hat and, without waiting to be thanked, had driven away.

Chapter Four

Tavy stood in the clearing, watching Willie Moser drive away. She felt dazed, light-headed with weariness and her body ached from the long, rough ride. Out of the trees the sun was bright. She blinked, shading her eyes as she gazed round her. After the immense space of the plains, the clearing seemed small, about the size of the garden in the middle of Cadogan Square, she reckoned. There were tree stumps in the grass, logs and branches scattered about and on one side was a newly dug patch, the earth still dark and moist. The Campions had not been here long, she thought — and there can't be many of them, not in a place this size, little more than a hut really, with sacking draped over the windows and a lop-sided chimney at one end. It was not at all what she had expected. But it must be the right place. Willie Moser had been told Tallangatta was the only property out this way. A property sounded large and grand. And fancy wanting a maidservant for such a small hut! Housework would be easy here.

There was no sign of anyone, no noise except for the clamour of birds in the surrounding trees; yet it didn't feel lonely, just sheltered and peaceful and warm. She picked up her bag and approached the hut. Then she stopped. What would Mrs. Campion think of her arriving like this in a torn dress, her hair every which way, her face streaked with dirt? She smoothed back her hair, tied on her bonnet, hitched up the rip in her skirt and, lifting her chin, walked resolutely up to the door. There was no bell, no knocker, only a rough wooden latch. She cleared her throat and thumped softly with her fist. The door creaked and moved inwards a fraction. The latch was unfastened. For a moment she listened, holding her breath. Silence. Then she tried again. This time the door opened just wide enough to look inside. In the dim light that filtered through the windows, she could see that the hut was empty. And it was dreadfully untidy. There was a table in the middle cluttered with dirty plates and mugs, tins, rope, candle stubs, a tinder box, a hatchet. There were charred sticks in the fireplace, a chair knocked sideways on the floor and garments lying here and there. Perhaps they did need a servant after all.

She sat down on her bag by the door and took off her shawl. The air was warm, like an English summer day. Insects buzzed in the grass, a bright green grass-hopper leapt suddenly over her foot and a swarm of flies seethed round a smelly bone lying nearby. The Campions must have a dog. She did hope they would come home soon for she had eaten nothing since the night before and her mouth felt parched with thirst. But the sun was still high above the trees. It might be hours before they returned. Perhaps they would not mind if she went inside. After all, she could tidy the place up a bit. It would be a surprise for them.

She gave the door a push and tiptoed over the bare earth floor, though there was nobody to disturb. Now she was inside, the hut seemed smaller than ever. She put down her bag and bundles and looked round for somewhere to hang her bonnet. There was very little furniture, no cupboards or hooks, just a few nails sticking out of the walls and a shelf above the hearth. And there was only one bed, a narrow bunk covered with rumpled blankets. There must be other rooms built on behind. She pulled aside the sacking from the back window and looked out at a patch of rough grass where a brown and white goat, tethered to a tree, was cropping the grass. There were some white cloths drying on a line, two buckets of water, a tin bowl standing on an upturned log, an axe, a spade, a heap of firewood; there was

37

a very small shed — the privy, she guessed — but there were no other rooms, no beds at all. I'll just have to sleep on the floor, she thought. Well, Mr. Jacob Pickering had warned her that Australia was no place for a weakling. This must be what he meant. As she turned away from the window she heard a noise, a soft cry that came from the corner by the fire. Cautiously she went closer, peering into the shadows. There was something in a wooden box, something alive was making a sort of whimpering sound. It might be a kitten or a puppy or . . . And then she saw that, lying on his back with his hands in the air, was a baby boy, about six months old. She was sure it was a boy, though it was hard to say why. There was something about his small round head, his firm chubby arms and legs that seemed to her decidedly masculine. She knelt down beside the box and held out her finger. The baby reached up and closed his own small fingers round it, looking up at Tavy with wide dark eyes.

"Hello." Tavy smiled at him. "You have been quiet. Have you just woken up?"

The baby made a gurgling noise and tugged her finger towards his mouth. It made Tavy laugh.

"Oh, you funny little thing," she said, touching his soft cheek. She had never had anything to do with babies before. At Saint Agatha's, the under three year olds had lived in a separate establishment and, although she had often helped Aunt Lavender with the juniors, they were always whining, squabbling, tumbling over, howling, and they were much too large and strugglesome to pick up and cuddle. Very gently, she pulled her finger from the baby's grasp and cradled her hands under his shoulders.

"Come on," she said, lifting him into her arms. "Let me have a look at you." The sunlight shone on his red gold hair as she carried him across the hut and laid him on the bed. "You're a little rascal," she told him, tenderly. "You're ever so wet."

He kicked his legs energetically as she pulled off his soggy napkin and, fearing he might roll off the bed, she moved him onto a blanket on the floor while she ran round to the back of the hut to fetch one of the cloths from the washing line. It took her a long time to fasten it on because the baby struggled and tried to roll over. She made faces at him and sang 'Twinkle, twinkle, little star' — her favourite nursery rhyme — but his face puckered and he started to cry. She bounced him up and down on the bed, but he continued to protest. He was probably hungry. It must be hours since his last feed. She knew that small babies, separated from their mothers, drank out of bottles but, although she searched, she couldn't find one. There was a jug of milk on the table, half a damper and a bit of hard, dry cheese. She poured some milk into a mug, smelling it to make sure it was not sour. Then, sitting the baby on her lap, she tilted it gently into his mouth. He made smacking noises with his lips, waving his arms excitedly so that most of the milk dribbled down his chin.

"You're starving, aren't you?" she said as she refilled the mug and the baby started to cry again.

She drank some herself, her tummy rumbling with emptiness. It tasted strange, fresh and creamy, but different. Of course, she thought, it must be goat's milk. When it was finished, she ate some cheese and a slice of damper, breaking off a piece for the baby, who gripped it tightly in his fist, sucking it contentedly. She watched him lying in a shaft of sunlight, wondering at his smooth, clear skin, his ears like little shells and his ridiculously small toes. She was so absorbed in looking after him that she forgot all about tidying the hut. She even forgot about the Campions' return until she heard the noise of horses' hoofs outside. They were back! What would they think, finding her here with the baby? She snatched him up but, before she could lay him back in his cradle box, heavy footsteps approached the hut and a man, carrying a gun, stood in the doorway. Tavy faced him, holding the baby protectively, and for a long moment they stared at each other. Was this Mr. Campion? Somehow she had not expected him to be so young and rough-looking. He ducked under the lintel, leaned his gun against the wall and tossed his hat on the table. He

39

seemed quite at home here. This must be Mr. Campion, her new Master.

"What are you doing with Joe?" His voice was gruff.

"Joe?"

"Yeah, the littl'un." He nodded towards the baby.

"Well, sir, he was crying so I gave him some milk. I hope I did right. I waited outside for a while, sir, but the door was unlatched so I came in. I'm Octavia Finch," she added in explanation. "I've come from Sydney." She paused, waiting for him to acknowledge her arrival, but without a word he came round the table and took Joe from her. She relinquished him unwillingly, her arms suddenly empty, feeling a twinge of envy at the look of tenderness on the Master's face as Joe tugged at his beard.

"How've you been, son?" He spoke gently now.

Son? Yes, seeing them together it was obvious. He had the same cast of features and his thick sandy hair had a reddish tinge.

"He's been happy as anything," she said. "It's lovely having a baby to look after — I mean, help to look after," she corrected herself, but he wasn't listening. She must remember her place. After all, even here she was only a servant. She would probably be expected to do the household chores while the Mistress took care of Joe. But where was she? Perhaps she was ill; or could it be that, like her own mother, she had died, for surely no woman would willingly leave her baby with only a young father to care for it? That would explain why the Master had engaged a servant. But it would also mean that, apart from Joe, she would be alone here with him. Where would she sleep? Supposing he turned out to be like Willie Moser, making advances and getting drunk? He seemed an uncouth type of man and he had hardly spoken to her. It had clearly annoyed him finding her with Joe, but wouldn't caring for him be part of her duties? Well, she would be glad to look after the poor little mite. In fact, she would love being a nurse maid instead of just a below stairs skivvy.

It would be worth putting up with the Master's rude

40

manner to live here, in this beautiful place, with little Joe. Not that she had any choice. It was too far to walk back to Burrawong Creek; besides, she would never find her way through the bush. It was four, no five, days' travel by coach to Sydney, and she had no money for her fare. She could not expect the Master to pay for a return trip if she refused to stay.

She waited till he had put Joe back in his box. Then, "What would you like me to do, sir?" she asked.

He glanced round at her. "Do?"

"What can I do to help you?"

"You aiming to stay, then?"

"Oh yes, sir," she said eagerly. "If you want me, that is. I've got a good character. You can be sure of that. I wouldn't be here if I hadn't, because I wouldn't have been considered suitable to come," she explained incomprehensibly. "Would you like to see my testimonial?"

Now he would tell her she was too young, too small and skinny for a rugged life in the outback. She lifted her chin and said "I'm ever so strong, sir, and I'm a hard worker. I don't mind what I turn my hand to. You'll always find me willing, sir."

She smiled at him, watching his face hopefully, but he turned away with a shrug, muttering inaudibly, and went outside.

She set about tidying the hut, picking up the scattered garments, hanging them on nails, straightening the blankets on the bed. Joe was gurgling contentedly to himself in the corner. She could see his small pink feet waving about above the edge of the box. It was hard to resist picking him up, but she did not want to displease the Master again. She collected the dirty dishes from the table so that she could wash them in the buckets behind the hut. Near the door, a dog was gnawing the smelly bone. It leapt up, snarling at her, and she ran in fright, dropping a knife. When she glanced back, she saw that the dog was tied to a tree stump. It growled, glaring at her with yellow eyes as she retrieved the knife. There was a horse grazing peacefully at the edge

41

of the clearing and she caught sight of the Master chopping
wood among the trees. She spent a long time scouring the
dishes, rubbing off the grease with a rag. When she carried
them back into the hut, the Master was kneeling by the
fireplace scraping the ashes together.

"I'll do that for you, sir," she said, putting the dishes
down on the table and hurrying to help him. "I always did
the fires in London."

"London, was it?" he said, laying kindling in the grate.
"That's a long way to come."

"Oh yes, it was a dreadfully long journey, but I was
determined to come and it only cost five pounds all the way
to Australia for a single woman with a good character, like I
told you, sir. Seems as how there's a shortage of women in
Australia because of all the men coming out to seek their
fortunes and the convicts and such. Most of the girls got
themselves jobs in Sydney, but I always wanted to live in the
country — space and fresh air, that's what I like, sir. London's ever so crowded and dirty and . . ."

He stood up and fetched the tinder box from the table.
She followed him, still talking.

"I don't mind being a long way from — well, a long way
from anywhere else. It was good of you to pay my fare from
Sydney to . . ."

"Pay your fare?" He faced her, the tinder box in his hand.

She nodded. "You did, sir." She paused. "Didn't you?"
Her voice faltered.

He knelt by the fireplace and set the kindling alight. They
both stared at the flames, flickering, growing, the smoke
curling upwards. "I never paid no fare," he said.

She stared at him, wide-eyed. "But the Employment
Officer in Sydney, he gave me the money you sent – five
shillings, it was — he said it was the usual arrangement,
really, sir." She spoke emphatically. "It was written in his
book and he gave me a slip of paper he'd signed with your
name and address on it. Campion . . ."

He shot up, glowering at her. "Don't call me that!"

She stepped back, alarmed by his vehemence. Then,

"Tallangatta?" she tried, her voice full of doubt.

"Campion's property, other side of the creek."

"But . . ." She hesitated. "In Burrawong Creek, they said it was the only house after the sign."

"They wouldn't know about this place. I've not been here that long."

Tavy nodded, understanding. Willie Moser had dropped her at the wrong place. No wonder this man had behaved strangely towards her. What must he think of her barging in, making herself at home, interfering with his baby son? She must go at once. She looked sadly towards the box in the corner, the small mound under the blanket, a tuft of red-gold hair. Would the Campions have a baby too? But it wouldn't be Joe. Oh, she didn't want to leave Joe.

She turned away with a sigh, fetched her bonnet and cape, collected her bundles and, picking up her bag, she faced the Master who was not her Master after all.

"It was all a mistake," she said in a small voice "I'm truly sorry, sir."

He shrugged, poking the fire with a stick so that it flared up, crackling.

"Please could you tell me the way to Tallangatta?"

"Back to the track, then on for a couple of miles. Take you a while to walk. Be dark before you get there. You could take a short cut over the creek and up the hill, but that's hard to find. I'll show you tomorrow."

Tomorrow? Did he mean her to stay the night? Where would she sleep? Somehow now that she was no longer a servant, the situation was different. It would be improper to share the hut with this rough young man.

"But, sir . . ."

"Not 'sir'." He frowned at her. "Jake's my name, Jake Drummond. You can stop here tonight. There's 'roo for supper." And, as if that settled the matter, he picked up his hat and went outside.

It was no use protesting. Without his directions, she would

never find the shortcut to Tallangatta, and she felt too tired to walk a long way and face her new employers that evening. Besides, she had noticed how suddenly darkness fell in the bush. Passengers in the coach had told stories of people losing their way and never being heard of again. So she stayed, scrubbing potatoes and turnips while Jake — it was difficult to think of him by his real name — milked the goat. She watched him from a distance, trying to see how he did it in case the Campions expected her to know. When she went back into the hut, he was sitting with his back to the door, holding Joe on his lap. She paused in the doorway, listening.

"Got a 'roo today, son; long range shot. That damn dog was onto it in no time. Nice young one, should be good eating. I'll have another go at hunting tomorrow. Come on, son, drink your milk."

He held a mug to Joe's mouth, but the baby's eyes were on Tavy. Jake glanced round. She smiled at him as she came in, but he turned away and she sensed his embarrassment.

"Would you like me to feed Joe?" she offered, dumping the vegetables on the table.

For a moment, he ignored Tavy, continuing to coax Joe with the mug. Then, as Joe gurgled, letting the milk dribble down his chin, Jake got up and held him out to her.

"Here. He's had enough. You can change him and put him to bed."

Left alone with Joe, she had played with him, sung 'Rock-a-bye-baby', dancing round the hut with him till he burped up his milk over her dress. She was just putting him back in his box when Jake came in with a great hunk of raw meat. She looked at it with disgust. Dead kangaroo, ugh! She gritted her teeth as she struggled to cut it up, but it sizzled in the pan, oozing succulent juice, and she forgot her revulsion for she felt hungry enough to eat anything.

It was beginning to grow dark when she went to the door to tell Jake it was ready. He was digging on the far side of the clearing and, as she walked over to him, the dog reared up, barking furiously. Jake turned round, yelling, "Stop that goddam noise," and then the sound of laughter came ringing through the air. It was that bird again, the bird which had woken her when she had been dreaming of Willie Moser. She could see it perched on a branch, grey-white with bright blue wings and a long beak. Then its mate flew over to join it, and together they sent their strange mocking laugh echoing across the clearing.

"What are those birds?" she asked, pointing to them.

"Kookaburras," he said, leaning on his spade. "Pair of 'em — come same time every evening."

"That's funny," Tavy said. "I didn't think birds could tell what time it was."

She looked up at the sky, remote and mysterious in the fading light. The birds were silent now, the dog lay still, she could feel the peace all around her. It was something she had sensed before when she had gazed at the sea, at the endless plains stretching away to the distant hills, often when she watched the sky. But always before, the feeling had stayed in the back of her mind, wordless, unidentified. Here she was conscious of it wrapping her round, real, almost tangible. Perhaps it was nature, the seasons, earth, wind, air, water — no, it was more than all those put together. Perhaps it was eternity, the world going round, timelessness.

"But time doesn't really matter here," she said. Then, realising that she had spoken aloud, she looked at Jake. He was watching her, but he immediately turned away, scraping the mud off his spade with a stick.

"Reckon it's time for tucker," he muttered.

"I've cooked the supper," she said.

He nodded and followed her to the hut.

They ate in silence. Tavy chewed the tough meat with determination, her eyes on her plate, although she could not help noticing how Jake shovelled in his food, spearing the meat with the tip of his knife. She smiled to herself, imagining what Mr. Lutterworth would have said, the sniffs and tongue-clicking that would have come from Cook and, of course, Aunt Lavender had been a stickler for good manners. But when you lived on your own, what did it matter? Were the Campions like him? She longed to ask but, after his angry reaction to the name, she was not going to mention it again. When he had finished his third helping and wiped his plate with damper, she poured him a mug of billy-tea. He pushed back his chair, stretched and loosened his belt.

"Tasty, that 'roo," he said.

Tavy nodded, her mouth full of gristle.

"Cooked good." He glanced at her approvingly and she felt herself blush. "She always burned everything," he muttered.

She? Who did he mean?

She carried her plate to the fire and discreetly got rid of the gristle. Then, from the protection of the shadows, "Who?" she asked.

Jake took a swig of tea. "Woman who lived here, Joe's mother." His voice was hard.

Tavy came back to the table. What had happened to her? Would he have used that tone of voice if she had died? She watched him get up and light the candle. It sputtered uncertainly, then the flame took shape. Shadows leapt up the rough wooden walls. Jake's eyes met her enquiring look as he came back to the table.

"She ran off," he muttered. "Three weeks ago, it was. Damned slut."

"But . . ." Tavy hesitated. "But if she was Joe's mother . . . I mean, he's such a dear baby. She couldn't just leave him."

Jake shrugged. "Good riddance. Joe and me's all right."

"But when he's bigger and crawling about, who'll look after him when you are out?"

"Dunno." He gripped a knife handle, scraping the blade along his sleeve.

Tavy sensed she had touched on a question that already worried him. Without a doubt, he was fond of Joe. For a while, neither of them spoke. Jake sat with his head in his hands. The fire hissed softly, Joe stirred in his box and outside a night bird called. Tavy's eyelids drooped, her limbs felt heavy with weariness. She longed to go to bed. Glancing up, she saw that he was watching her. Something in his expression disturbed her and she got to her feet and began to collect the dishes.

He touched her arm. "Leave 'em. Time for bed."

She drew back. "Would it be all right if I slept on the floor? Or I don't mind sleeping outside. I used to sleep on deck when I was in the ship. I liked it; it was cool and I could watch the stars and . . ." The words tumbled out, to cover her confusion.

"You have the bed."

She avoided his eye. "Oh no, I couldn't possibly take your bed. Where'll you sleep?"

He shrugged, giving her a sideways look. She moved away and knelt beside her carpet bag, fumbling with the clasp. After a moment, he picked up the candle and went outside. She stood, holding her breath, listening to his footsteps going round to the back of the hut. Then, hurriedly, she gathered an armful of blankets from the bed and spread them on the floor close to Joe's box. She would spend the night there. If she was quick, she could be asleep — or appear to be — before Jake came back. She pulled off her boots and stockings, then, barefoot, she tiptoed to the door. She stared into the darkness, trying to locate his whereabouts. The dog slept in the grass, leaves rustled in the wind, tree frogs hummed a steady note — but Jake? No, she couldn't hear him. She glanced up at the stars. Please make it all right, she prayed silently as she padded back to the fire and unbuttoned her bodice. It was risky to undress, but her clothes felt stiff with dirt and if she was quick . . .

She pulled her dress over her head and rummaged in her bag for her nightgown. She hadn't worn it for several nights. It must be buried at the bottom, but in the dim light it was hard to see. She tossed out garments in growing desperation. There was a sound behind her. She sprang round, her heart thumping, clasping her arms across her chest. Jake stared at her, his face shadowed above the candle flame.

47

"How dare you!" She snatched up a blanket and hugged it round her, trembling with indignation and fear. First that night in Sydney, then Willie Moser, and now this.

Jake put the candle-stick on the table and sat on the bed, tugging at his boots. Now he was going to undress. Clutching the blanket round her, she darted to the door and ran out into the darkness. Behind the hut, she splashed cold water on her burning face, her arms and neck, dabbing herself dry with her petticoat. Then she crept back and waited, close to the door, shivering in the chilly wind. She stared upwards and the stars seemed to grow bigger and brighter in the inky sky. She could hear Jake moving about, poking the fire, murmuring. Was he saying his prayers? Talking to Joe? At last the candle went out, she heard a creak and a thump as he got into bed and soon there was the sound of deep, steady breathing. Cautiously she slipped back into the hut, lay down on the floor by Joe and slept.

Tavy sat up and brushed the hair out of her eyes. A shaft of brightness shone through the half-open door, a cacophony of bird calls came from outside. It was morning. She had slept right through the night in the same room as that rough, uncouth man — and Joe. Pushing off the blankets, she peered into his box. It was empty. She pulled on her dress and padded barefoot to the door. A few feet away, Jake was sitting on the grass, holding Joe between his knees.

"Hello," she said, stepping outside.

The dog started to bark. Jake glanced at her. "Stop that noise," he shouted at the dog.

"It's a lovely morning!" Tavy looked up at the sun, screwing up her eyes. "I'm afraid I overslept."

Jake didn't answer. He picked a long grass and held it towards Joe, who reached out for it, batting it with his hands.

"Clever boy," said Tavy, squatting on her heels beside Jake. Distracted from the grass, Joe gazed at her with large dark eyes.

"You are a clever boy, aren't you?" she said, smiling and wiggling her fingers at him. Joe made excited bouncing movements, showing off in front of his audience. Tavy laughed.

"He's got such a funny little nose," she said. "It's like a pink button."

She glanced at Jake, wondering if he would think her insulting, but he was watching Joe, his head half turned away from her. She sensed that he was avoiding her eye. Was he annoyed at her intrusion, or embarrassed at having seen her in her petticoat? But, judging by the way he had stared that had not been her impression last night.

The dog started to whine, tugging at its rope, and Jake stood up, saying, "Come on, son. There's work to be done."

"Shall I take him for you?" Tavy offered, but Jake walked past her into the hut without an answer. She waited, listening to Joe's wails. If only she could stay with him, stay in this peaceful, timeless place and look after him. But then there was Jake. With Jake, it was impossible. And she had been engaged by the Campions. They had paid her fare from Sydney. She was committed to go to Tallangatta. All the same, when Jake came out again carrying his gun, she stood in front of him so that he had to listen to her.

"Please," she began. He frowned at her. "I just wondered, that is, if you like, I could stay with Joe while . . ."

"Joe's all right," he growled.

"Oh yes, I know. It's just that I thought I could do something to help before I go to Tallangatta."

Jake shrugged. "I can manage." He dodged past Tavy and started to cross the clearing. She watched him go, hurt and angry at his rebuff. He was ill-mannered and uncouth and she didn't like him at all. The sooner she left, the better.

She ran after him, calling, "You'll have to show me the way. I can't go if I don't know the way, can I?" She could be rude as well.

He walked on without looking at her. "To Campion's?"

"Yes."

"Back to the track, then on that way." He swung round, pointing behind the hut.

49

"But you told me there was a short cut."

He glanced at her impatiently.

"Please, if you could show me the short way."

He stopped abruptly. "Down to the creek where I get the water."

"But I don't know where that is."

"Come on." With a jerk of his head, he turned back towards the hut. She followed him, lifting her skirts as she hopped over the tussocks of grass. She wished she could put on her boots, but Jake was already heading off to the right of the hut where the ground sloped gently down through the trees. A narrow path wound between bushes starred with white flowers, which smelled of honey as she brushed past them. Underfoot, sharp twigs and dry leaves pricked her tender bare feet.

"Wait for me," she shouted. "I haven't got my boots on."

But Jake did not appear to have heard, for he charged ahead and Tavy lost sight of his hat amongst the bushes. At the bottom of the slope, she caught up with him standing beside the creek. Sunlight filtering through the leaves sparkled on the clear water.

"Oh, it's lovely!" Tavy said.

The creeks they had crossed driving over the plains had been turgid and brown. Jake pointed to a shallow stretch where the stream bubbled over bright pebbles.

"You can get over there," he said. "Then go up to the top. You'll see Campion's place over to the left soon as you come through the trees. There's paddocks, fenced in, orchards and such like. All the buildings are on beyond that."

"Buildings?" Tavy asked. "Is it big?"

Jake shrugged. "Dunno," he said. "Never been there." And he turned and climbed up the path to the hut.

It seemed strange that Jake had never been to Tallangatta. The Campions were neighbours, his only neighbours. Had they never invited him there? Or had he refused to go? He was certainly not a friendly man. When she reached the clearing, taking her time for her feet and ankles were painfully scratched, he was buckling the saddle on his horse. She watched him mount, keeping well clear of the dog who, released from its rope, was whining impatiently round the horse's legs. He must be going hunting. She had heard him tell Joe he was going today. She wondered whether to say good-bye. But he'll only ignore me again, she thought, and he'll be glad I'm not here when he comes back. All the same, when he twisted round to adjust the gun slung over his back, he caught sight of her standing by the hut. She raised her arm in a hesitant wave. For a moment, their eyes met. He nodded, unsmiling, then, turning back, he urged the horse forward and rode away.

Joe was awake when Tavy went back into the hut. He began to cry mournfully and without conviction, as soon as he heard her moving about. She spoke to him gently as she put on her stockings and boots.

"Poor little lamb, don't fret."

She reminded herself of Aunt Lavender. "It's all right, Joe. I'm here."

But she wouldn't be here long. He would be on his own, abandoned for hours with no one to feed him, change him, play with him. She picked him up and sat him on her lap for a drink of milk. He dribbled it down his chin, batting at the mug with his fists.

"All right, you little rascal," she said. "I haven't had any breakfast." And she drank it herself. While she changed him, he sucked his thumb, his eyelids drooping with sleep. "You're tired," she told him as she tucked him in his box. "Have a good nap."

When she had washed his nappy, as well as a pair of Jake's socks, a shirt and two other nappies and hung them out to dry, she cleared up the supper dishes and tidied the hut. Really, Jake did need someone to help him. He was so untidy and with Joe to look after . . .

She went to his box in the corner and gazed down at him with an ache in her heart. If only, if only — but it was no use. She had to go to the Campions. Sadly she turned away, picked up her belongings and, closing the door of the hut behind her, she set off for Tallangatta.

Chapter Five

"If you please, miss, is this Tallangatta?"

"Yes." The tall girl standing in the doorway looked down at Tavy. "Who are you?"

"I'm Octavia Finch, ma'am." She bobbed a jerky curtsy. It was difficult holding her carpet bag. "The Employment gentleman in Sydney sent me," she explained, smiling at the girl. "And before that, I came from London in the *Henrietta*." She wanted no misunderstanding this time.

The girl regarded Tavy without smiling, her eyes moving disdainfully over Tavy's muddy boots, the strands of hair escaping from her bonnet, her torn skirt. Tavy lifted her chin and looked back unflinchingly, but she felt her cheeks burn, conscious of the girl's pretty gown and her glossy black ringlets tied with blue ribbons.

"You had better come and see Mama," the girl said and she turned and led the way along a passage, her slippers tripping neatly over the patterned runner.

Mama? So this must be Miss Campion, Tavy thought, glancing at the gilt-framed pictures on the walls. There were pictures like that at Cadogan Square and the smell was the same — beeswax, wood smoke, tobacco. But from the outside, this single storey house of white painted wood was very different. She had approached it from the back, having walked half way round before she had noticed the steps up to the verandah and found the front door. But it had given her an opportunity to see how big a place Tallangatta was. The buildings covered a wide area. Separated from the main homestead, beyond two large waterholes, was a wool shed and what looked like a farm with poultry, horses and cows. The other buildings were clustered together, some made of split logs like Jake's, some less crudely constructed of wooden planks or stone.

It was quiet and peaceful in the morning sun and there did not seem to be anyone about, though through a window Tavy glimpsed a stout woman asleep in a rocking chair. She heard someone singing and the swish of a broom on a hard floor and she did see a man in the distance as she came through the paddocks, a labourer she had guessed from his rough clothes. He had walked away without noticing her into an enclosure full of sheep, and she had gone on through an orchard of fruit trees, their blossom dropping on the thick green grass. It's spring here, she had reminded herself, spring in September, and nearer the house she had come to a garden full of flowers. There were geraniums, she knew those, pansies and daffodils, and many, many others she had never seen before.

It was flowers — a formally arranged vase of yellow and white — that Tavy first noticed when the girl opened a door at the end of the passage and beckoned her in. The rest of the room seemed dark. It was musty, airless and heavily curtained, cluttered with furniture, ornaments and knick-knacks. The walls were almost completely hidden by pictures and an assortment of oriental rugs lay on the floor.

"The new maidservant is here, Mama," the girl said.

A woman, seated at a writing table under the window, rose and came towards them. She was shorter than her daughter, with a dumpy figure.

"Well, well," she said, looking at Tavy for a moment with a slight smile.

Tavy smiled back, relieved to see the new Mistress had a gentle face.

"Good day, ma'am," she said, with a quick bob.

"This is a surprise," Mrs. Campion said kindly. "It is many months since I applied to Sydney for another girl to

53

come and help us. What is your name?"

"Octavia Finch, ma'am."

"We are glad to have you, Octavia."

"I'm ever so glad to be here, ma'am," Tavy said eagerly. "I like the countryside. I was in London before I came to Australia. It was a good position, in a high class establishment, and it wasn't that I got my notice, ma'am," she assured Mrs. Campion earnestly. "It was just that I've spent all my life in London and it's so crowded and dirty. We had fogs all winter and rain all spring and . . . "

"Spring," Mrs. Campion interrupted her sadly. "Spring in England, that is something I miss most of all. Woods full of bluebells, primroses . . ."

"Our garden is full of flowers, Mama," her daughter remarked, turning her back on Tavy and picking out notes on the upright piano.

"Indeed you are right, Louisa," Mrs. Campion agreed. "We are most fortunate here, even though we are so isolated. We have made Tallangatta quite a self-contained little community. It is essential to do so in a place where one has no neighbours. I hope you will be happy with us, Octavia."

"Oh, yes, ma'am, I'm sure I will be but . . ." Tavy hesitated. Didn't they know about Jake? He was a neighbour. She glanced at Louisa, who was twisting her ringlets with a bored expression. Perhaps it would be better not to mention him.

"Now, Louisa will take you to meet Mrs. O'Rourke and Lily," Mrs. Campion said.

Louisa banged down the piano lid and, without looking at Tavy, she opened the door and went out. With her heavy bag, her cape and bonnet, it was difficult to keep up with Louisa, who walked quickly back along the passage to a side door. They went through the garden, across a courtyard, round a corner, under an archway, on and then on again until Tavy wondered if Louisa would ever stop. At last, flinging open the door of a cottage, she called "Lily!" There was no answer. She called again and, when there was still no

54

response, she slammed the door shut and went back the way they had come. Tavy panted after her. The sun was warm, she felt hot and dishevelled, her arm ached from carrying her bag. Then, rounding a corner, Louisa almost collided with a girl carrying a laundry basket.

"Oh, Miss Louisa, I didn't see you coming!" she exclaimed. She was large, with a round rosy face. Her dress was stretched in tight wrinkles over her plump bosom and her cap was almost hidden by a profusion of yellow curls.

"There you are, Lily," said Louisa crossly. "This is the new servant. Mama says to take her to Mrs. O'Rourke."

"Very good, Miss Louisa." Lily looked at Tavy with interest, then, glancing at Louisa's retreating figure, she stuck out her tongue. "That's what I think of her," she said with a giggle. "You might as well know from the start. Tries to queen it over everyone, she does. The rest of them's not too bad, and as for Harry . . ." She paused. "Well, you'd better come and meet Mrs. O'Rourke."

Mrs. O'Rourke, the cook, turned out to be the woman Tavy had seen asleep. She was in the kitchen, a separate building behind the house, stirring a saucepan over a large open range.

"So you're a Londoner, are you?" she said, in her strong Irish brogue, when Tavy explained who she was. "Yes, you're as skinny as a little cock sparrow."

"Everyone tells me that," Tavy said, thinking of Duggan and Mrs. Trumper.

"Well, if I can't fatten you up, no one can. I'm a good cook, I am." She banged the spoon on the edge of the pan as if to underline her statement.

It was true, as Tavy soon discovered. At dinner time, Mrs. O'Rourke placed a generous plateful of food in front of her.

"There," she said, "and mind you eat every scrap."

After nothing but the remains of Joe's milk for breakfast, Tavy was glad to obey.

When the meal was over, Lily went off to the house to clear the dining room.

"No, not you." Mrs. O'Rourke put out a restraining hand as Tavy made a move to follow. "The Mistress won't want two of you there, chattering and disturbing the Master. You can get on with the dishes," she added, lowering herself into her rocking chair. "I have to rest after my meal. I'm a martyr to my stomach." She pulled a bottle from under the cushion, drew out the cork and tilted it to her mouth. "Physic," she explained, putting a hand to her diaphragm and leaning back with a pained expression.

"Poor Mrs. O'Rourke," Tavy said sympathetically. Aunt Lavender had also suffered from a delicate digestion.

Lily, coming in with a tray of dishes, paused, looked at Mrs. O'Rourke and then gave Tavy a wink.

"Proper old tippler, she is," Lily told Tavy that night. They were sharing a bedroom in the staff cottage.

"But she said . . ." Tavy started.

Lily giggled. "Don't you believe it. She's got a stomach like a horse. She eats far more than Master Harry, and he's got a real man's appetite."

She lay back on the bed and sighed deeply. Tavy glanced at her.

"What's he like?" she asked, her curiosity aroused.

"Well," Lily gazed dreamily at the ceiling, "he's tall and he's got black hair and he's ever so dashing. You wait till you see him. He's away just now, off round the property. There always seems to be some sort of trouble — scabby mouth or floods or drought, then the 'roos eat all the grass and the dingoes kill the sheep and . . ."

"Dingoes?"

"Wild dogs, horrible great beasts, they are," Lily said. "When I was little, they used to come right into Gunderra township. You could hear them howling; real scary, it was. Then there's the Abos."

"What are they?" Tavy asked.

"Abos?" Lily laughed. "Natives. Aborigines. Don't you know anything?"

"'Course I do," Tavy protested. "They eat their babies." She remembered Cook saying that at Cadogan Square.

"Eat sheep, more likely," said Lily. "They're always after sheep. They move around, stop where there's a water hole till it dries up, then they move on. They camp by the creeks in the summer when it's hot."

Creeks, Tavy thought. Jake's hut was close to a creek. What about Joe?

"There's a creek down the hill, isn't there?" she asked.

"That's right." Lily sat up and started to unpin her cap. "It marks the border of the Tallangatta property."

Tavy watched Lily shake out her hair, wondering whether to ask her about Jake. It seemed strange that no one had yet mentioned their closest neighbour.

"Who owns the land the other side of the creek?" she asked casually.

"Nobody." Lily tugged a brush through her tangled curls. "There's some bushman who's built himself a hut. And d'you know what?" She opened her eyes wide. "He had a woman there with him and a baby too. But she went off with some traveller who stopped for the night, two or three weeks ago. She rode off on the back of his horse. Sam saw her go."

"Who's Sam?"

"He's the stockman. He told Mrs. O'Rourke that she was a real slut, but I wouldn't fancy living with that fellow. Sam says he's a bad-tempered brute."

"Have you seen him?" Tavy asked.

Lily tossed back her hair. "No, I've never been down to the creek. It's an awful steep climb coming up again. My legs would give out." She giggled and slapped her thighs. "Think I'm too fat?" she asked, looking at her legs.

"No, not really." Tavy wasn't interested in Lily's size. "D'you think he'll stay there?"

"Who?"

"The man by the creek."

"Oh, him. No, I shouldn't think so. Master Harry says he'll be in trouble when the Lands Commissioner comes round because he hasn't got a licence for that run of land."

"Perhaps he'll get one," Tavy said. She didn't want Jake to

take Joe away.

"Not if Master Harry can help it. He wants the run for Tallangatta. He looks after the whole property now the Master can't work."

"What happened to the Master?"

"He had a riding accident — about two years ago, it was. He was right out in the bush when his horse shied at a 'roo; he fell and hurt his back real bad. He was ill for ever such a long time. The Mistress was beside herself with worry. He did get better, though he can't hardly walk now. She's got him one of them chairs with wheels, but he stays in his study most of the time, writing up the accounts and keeping the books and such like. Nobody's allowed to make a noise near his room."

"Mr. Campion needs constant rest and quiet," the Mistress told Tavy next day, before taking her to the study to meet him. "He does not appreciate feminine chatter," she added pointedly.

Tavy followed the Mistress into the small room on tiptoe. She stood with her lips pressed together, bobbing a curtsy when she was introduced to the Master. He was sitting in a deep leather arm chair, a big, shaggy-haired man with a strong, lined face. A black and white dog lay asleep beside him. Tavy looked at his large bony hands holding the ledger on his lap, trying to imagine him as a young settler like Jake. She felt his eyes on her; they were deep-set, discerning.

"My wife tells me you're a city girl." He spoke in a low, gravelly voice. "You'll soon get used to living out here. Either you like it or you don't." He glanced at his wife. There was a moment's pause and Tavy sensed the tension between them as the Mistress looked away, touching a book on the desk.

"I came here over thirty years ago," the Master went on. "It was wild, undiscovered country. I worked hard to make something of it, I can tell you."

Tavy nodded solemnly. There was a powerful air of authority about the Master.

"Tallangatta's one of the finest properties west of Gunderra. We've got fifteen thousand head of sheep, cattle, horses, crops — place is thriving. But it doesn't run itself and I'm not able to get about." He paused, frowning. "My son, Harry, looks after it now, has done for two years, since he was seventeen. You met Harry?" There was pride in his voice.

Tavy shook her head. "No, sir."

"You will," said the Master. "He'll be back before long."

The next day, Tavy saw a tall man coming towards her across the courtyard. He was young and dark and —yes, Lily was right, he was ever so dashing. It was Harry. He walked straight past Tavy, stopped, swung round and stared at her.

"Good day, sir." She bobbed a curtsy.

"What are you doing here?"

"I'm the new maid, sir."

"What's happened to Lily?"

"Oh, she's still here, sir."

"Good." He turned and walked on.

Tavy watched his long-legged, confident swagger. It was not only his height and colouring that were like Louisa's. He was rude as well, with the same arrogance. Think a lot of yourself, don't you? Tavy said to his back view. You're bound to, I suppose, when your father lets you run a big place like this. He's proud of you too. I could tell from his voice; and I'll wager the Mistress and Louisa spoil you. As for that Lily — but perhaps you've got your eye on her. You certainly did not pay any heed to me, did you? Was Lily still here? That was all you could say. Yes, Tavy thought, going on across the courtyard, Harry liked things all his own way. Jake would have to take care if Harry had made up his mind to add Jake's run to the Tallangatta property. She did not mind about Jake. She had seen enough of his crude man-

59

ners to know what kind of man he was. No wonder his woman had gone off and left him. But she had gone without Joe. How could she have done that? He was such a darling baby. Oh, but I'm glad she did, Tavy thought with a sudden longing to see him again. At least he was not very far away.

Through the rest of the day, she kept remembering him, his little round head, his small hands clutching her finger, his ridiculous nose. That night, alone in the bedroom— Lily had disappeared somewhere after they had washed up the dishes – Tavy stood in the open doorway, staring out into the darkness. The stars were very bright, myriads of light points piercing the sky. She stepped outside, tiptoeing barefoot on the hard ground, through the courtyard to the orchard gate. Beyond the paddocks, the land sloped down towards the creek. Perhaps she would be able to catch a glimmer of light from Jake's candle in the hut. For a while, she scanned the dense black trees, but there was nothing to be seen. It was hidden, far away.

She glanced up at the stars. "Look after Joe," she whispered aloud before she ran back to the cottage. Lily would probably be there by now, wondering where she was. But the room was empty and Tavy fell asleep before Lily came back.

"Where were you?" she asked Lily in the morning.

Lily smiled mysteriously. "That'd be telling," was all she said.

For the next few days, as the strangeness of life at Tallangatta began to wear off, Tavy found herself thinking more and more about Joe. She pictured him lying in his wooden box, alone in the hut, and she longed to see him again. The trouble was she seemed to have no free time, and there was nearly two weeks to wait until her afternoon off. "Every other Sunday you may take a half holiday," the Mistress had told her, but "I'm off this Sunday," Lily had stated firmly. She had to work hard. Lily was only too glad to share her duties and Mrs. O'Rourke refused to do anything but cook. "I did not come all this way from Dublin to scour and scrub," she announced whenever there was a sink full of dirty dishes or a basket of vegetables to be peeled.

The day started early; there was the house to be cleaned, washing to be laundered, floors to be scrubbed. Lily sang as she worked; hymn tunes, folk songs, some with rude words she had learned from the shepherds, nursery rhymes, anything that came into her head. "Reckon I sound better than her in there," she said to Tavy, nodding towards the drawing room where, each morning, Louisa practised on the upright piano. She played scales, up and down, faltering, stopping, then off again, up and down. She sang too, in a shrill soprano voice which cracked on the top notes. "Sounds like a sick cow," Lily remarked and she and Tavy giggled together. Music, with French and English literature, was part of Louisa's tuition, supervised by her mother. "What's the use of all that learning living out here in the bush?" said Lily.

Before the mid-day meal, there was the table to set in the dining room with a clean cloth, polished glass and silver, for, as Lily said, "Madam's ever so particular about it being just so". When Lily rang the gong, the Mistress or Harry, if he was home, wheeled the Master into the dining room and the family stood, with bowed heads, while he said the grace.

At first, Tavy only helped Lily carry the trays of food across to the house, scuttling back to the kitchen while Lily waited at the table. "I've never done parlourmaid's work before," she said to Mrs. O'Rourke. "You'll soon learn," Mrs. O'Rourke told her. "You can give Lily a hand in a day or so."

In the afternoons, while Mrs. O'Rourke slept off her indigestion and the Master rested in his study, the Mistress read aloud to Louisa while she sewed her sampler. On fine days, they sat in the garden to sketch and paint — Louisa had a box of water colours that had been sent from England — and sometimes they went for a drive in the spring cart, with Bron, the old black and white dog, padding along

61

behind. Provided all the work had been finished, Lily and Tavy were free until tea time, but on washing days there was the ironing to be done.

"There's an awful lot of it," Tavy said the first day, as they unpegged the dry clothes from the line.

"Oh, this won't take long," Lily said airily. "We'll share it." She picked out a few garments. "I'll do the shirts and petticoats and you can do the linen. That's nice and simple, no tucks and pleats."

Tavy eyed the basket doubtfully. Dora had done the ironing at Cadogan Square.

Lily finished hers quickly, smoothing rhythmically, gophering the frills. But whatever Tavy pressed turned out wrinkled and creased. She damped and redamped, testing the flat iron with a drop of water the way Lily did. Even so, ugly brown scorch marks appeared on the sheets so that she had to rub them with lemon juice and put them to soak. The next day there was another basketful waiting to be done.

"Practice makes perfect. You'll soon find it easy," Lily said breezily, folding her last camisole. "Well, I'm off to put my feet up."

Tavy gritted her teeth and kept at it. If Lily could press all those pleats and frills, she was not going to be defeated by pillow cases and napkins. Besides, it had occurred to her that although the linen might be easier to iron, Lily was not unaware that there was also a great deal more of it. As soon as she was more proficient, they would share it out more fairly. At last, on the third afternoon, she began to find it easier. There had been no washing that morning to add to the pile, and by tea time the basket was empty at last.

The next day it rained, a steady damping drizzle. "No washing today," Tavy said cheerfully. She would go and see Joe. But would the rain keep Jake at home? Well, she could soon tell. If his horse was in the clearing, she would come back again. Don't let him be there, don't let him be there. The words went round in her head as she polished the bedroom floors.

The moment the dinner dishes were done, she raced

back to the cottage for her cape, slipping out again quickly before Lily saw her. The rain had stopped. Clouds raced across the sky, billowing like the *Henrietta's* sails. As she went through the orchard, drops showered on her head and her skirt was soon soaked from the long wet grass. She hoped no one would notice her go into the paddocks. There had been a man there before and she knew now that it had been the stockman, Sam. He wore one of those cabbage tree hats of plaited straw, like Jake's, though Sam kept his jammed right down over his nose. It almost seemed to be part of his head. He had been in the kitchen several times with Mrs. O'Rourke but, as soon as she and Lily had appeared, he had shambled off, tucking a bottle under his coat. He lived alone in one of the outlying huts, but she had noticed him about the place, watching her out of the corner of his eye. It was Sam who had known about Jake's woman. She had the feeling that he did not miss much.

She unlatched the gate, closing it carefully behind her. There were ewes with young lambs in the enclosed sheep pens, but no sign of Sam. Once through the lower gate, she was hidden in the bushes. There was a fresh smell of wet leaves, eucalyptus and blossom, a clamour of birds, small bright parakeets and great white cockatoos with yellow crests that rose about the trees with a strident cry. The path was hard to follow and, when she reached the creek, she found herself in a different place. Slithering in the mud, she made her way along the bank to the shallow stretch where she had crossed before. It was deeper after the rain, but her boots and stockings were wet through already. As she stepped onto the far bank, she felt a tingle of excitement. Silly, she told herself. I'm only going to see little Joe. At least, I hope I am. Oh, I do hope I am. Oh, don't let Jake be there.

She stopped when she reached the edge of the trees. There was the goat, the privy, the pile of logs, the water buckets, and beyond the hut she could see Jake's horse on the far side of the clearing. He was there! She had come so near and now it was no good. She might as well just turn round and go back again. But she stayed where she was, staring down at the hut, the goat, the privy, the water buckets, as if she could will Jake to go away. There was a window at the back of the hut. If she pulled aside the sacking, she could look in and see Joe. Cautiously she started to go across the grass. Any moment, Jake might come round the corner and see her. He would stand and stare at her, silent and hostile. And that would be that.

But he didn't come, and she ran the last few steps to the little window, tugged back the corner of the sacking and peered in. The dim interior seemed small and crude after the well-furnished formality of the Tallangatta house. She could see Joe's box by the fireplace, his small hands waving above the edge. Then the door opened and Jake came in. She ducked out of sight, holding her breath. She could hear his boots clomp across the floor, his voice speaking softly, "Go to sleep now, son. Rain's stopped. I'll get on with chopping that tree I felled." There were more footsteps, the creak of the door. Tavy peeped through the window again. Jake had gone. She crept along the side wall of the hut until she could see the clearing. Jake was walking away through the trees with an axe over his shoulder. She watched him till he was out of sight. In a moment, she heard the thwack as his axe bit into the wood. He wasn't likely to come back for a while. It would be safe for her to pop in and see Joe. She turned the corner, started towards the door and stopped abruptly. The dog. She had forgotten about the dog. It was watching her, its ears pricked. Tavy took a step nearer and it sprang up, a rumbling growl in its throat. She stared into its yellow eyes and edged forward another foot. The growl grew louder, more menacing, and it began to stalk towards her. She backed, keeping pace with the dog until, jerked to a halt at the end of its rope, it broke into ferocious barking. In seconds Tavy was round the back of the hut, across the grass, into the trees, then running down to the creek, skidding on the damp leaves. Half way, she caught her foot in a tree root and tumbled forward. She sat up, gasping for breath, and for a moment she stayed there rubbing her knees. No need to hurry now, she thought. Jake couldn't see me, even if he does come back to the hut to discover why the dog's barking. And she got to her feet, shook the twigs from her cape and went on slowly, picking sprigs of white blossom.

"Good heavens, girl, wherever have you been?" Mrs. O'Rourke rounded on Tavy with red-faced disapproval. She placed a tray of hot scones on the kitchen table.

"I just went for a walk." She held out the flowers. "Look, aren't they lovely?"

Mrs. O'Rourke ignored the flowers. "You're covered in mud. Better clean yourself up before tea. The Mistress'll be having a fit if she sees you like that."

"But Lily serves the tea, not me."

"She'll need help today. Master Harry's come back early and he's always starving."

"Well, can I have a mug or something to put my bunch in?"

"Don't fuss with those now. Go and clean yourself up," Mrs. O'Rourke told her. "Ah, here's Lily. Cut that fruit cake in slices, Lily, and lay it out nice on this plate."

"But they'll die," Tavy persisted. "And they smell so sweet." She held the flowers under Lily's nose.

"That's wedding bunch," Lily said. "It's ever so romantic." She giggled.

Tavy glanced at her. She had brushed her curls so that they fluffed out round her face, and changed into a clean dress and apron. Her cheeks were flushed and her eyes shone.

"Wedding bunch," Tavy said. "What a pretty name."

"It won't be a pretty name I'll be calling you, my girl," threatened Mrs. O'Rourke, "unless you . . ."

But Tavy had already run out of the door. She changed quickly into her other dress. It was faded and frayed, the skirt bunched lopsidedly where she had stitched up the tear, but at least it was clean. She wiped the mud off her boots and combed her hair. It was straight and brown, a nondescript mouse. She had never minded about its colour before, but suddenly she envied Lily her golden curls. Louisa had nice hair too, dark and glossy, neatly groomed. She pinned on her cap with a sigh and ran to help Lily.

Tea was served in the drawing room, although the Master preferred to stay in his study. Harry was seldom home in time, but today he stood leaning nonchalantly against the mantelpiece, one leg across the other, talking to his mother and Louisa, who sat demurely on the couch with Bron, the old sheepdog, at their feet. He still wore his working clothes, high boots, moleskin trousers and a leather waistcoat over an open-neck shirt, but there was a stylish elegance about him. Tavy noticed him glance at her as she carried in the teapot. She was just following Lily out again when the Mistress called her back.

"Octavia, ask Mrs. O'Rourke for a jug of hot water, please."

"Yes, ma'am." She curtsied and, as she closed the door behind her, she heard Harry say, "Well, I suppose they can't all be beauties."

She paused, her hand on the door knob.

"Tch, Harry, not so loud," the Mistress said.

There was a titter from Louisa. "But Mama, it isn't just her looks; her clothes are a disgrace."

"Why not give her some of your gowns, Louisa?" Harry's voice was teasing. "You have a devilish large amount for life in the bush."

"I happen to mind about my appearance, my dear Harry, even if . . ."

Tavy did not wait to hear more. She tiptoed away down the passage, her fists clenched indignantly. What unkind things to say! She couldn't help her shabby clothes. She only had two dresses of dark grey cotton, because that was the rule at Saint Agatha's, and the uniform at Cadogan Square had been firmly rounded up by Cook for her replacement. It was all very well for Louisa, with her wardrobe full of pretty gowns. But it was Harry's first remark that stung her most. "Can't all be beauties," meaning she was plain and skinny and small. And Lily was a beauty. So he had an eye for Lily, did he? Certainly she fancied him. That was quite clear. Well, if Lily liked men who were conceited and spoilt, that was her affair. She didn't care what Harry thought of her. It didn't concern her one little bit. Joe was the person she minded about and tomorrow she would go and see him again.

Chapter Six

"Tavy. Tavy."

As she came through the orchard, she heard someone calling her. It was Lily. Tavy caught sight of her bright hair through the trees. She was standing by the gate that led to the garden.

"What happened to you?" she asked. "It's ever so late."

"Is it?" Tavy was surprised. She looked at the sky. It had been a sunless day, with bouts of rain and lowering cloud. She had not noticed that it was getting dark.

"The Mistress has been asking for you. She told me to find you. Sam said he'd seen you go past the sheep pens a while ago."

"Sam?"

"Yes, the stockman. Come on," she urged, turning and hurrying along the narrow garden path with Tavy behind her. "Where've you been?"

"Oh, down the hill," Tavy said vaguely. "I like it in the woods."

"You'd best take care. There's snakes and red back spiders and funnel webs and the magpies attack you when they're nesting and . . ."

"What does the Mistress want?" Tavy interrupted, ignoring Lily's catalogue of dangers.

"Don't know. But I'd go quick if I was you."

Thoughts raced round Tavy's head as she crossed the courtyard to the house. What had she done? Scorched the sheets, broken something precious, forgotten to empty the slops — there were so many things it could be. Supposing she was given her notice. Where would she go? To the hut, to little Joe? But there was Jake as well, and she couldn't stay in the hut with him. He had been out that afternoon with his horse and the dog, and she had spent a blissful few hours with Joe, feeding him, changing him, talking and singing to him while he sat on her lap. She had rinsed out his dirty nappies and washed his clothes, throwing in a few garments of Jake's just because, well, she was a little bit sorry for him with all the extra woman's work he had to do. And then she had tidied up the hut and swept the floor — for Joe's sake, she told herself. Too much dust lying about was bad for babies. When it was done, she had risked staying a little longer and taken Joe outside for a walk in the fresh air. She had carried him round the clearing, telling him about the birds and the tall gum trees, the fluffy yellow wattle that was starting to wither. There had been no sun, but it was beautiful all the same and she had been conscious of the peace, the timelessness she had noticed before. Perhaps that was why she had stayed so long, strangely unconcerned about Jake's return. But he had not come back and, when Joe had dropped off to sleep, she had closed the door carefully and walked slowly back determining to go to the hut whenever she could.

The sound of the piano came from the drawing room. She waited a moment outside the door. The music stopped, there were voices, laughter. Harry was there too. She took a deep breath and knocked. The Mistress answered and, as Tavy went in, she looked up from her sewing.

"Octavia — at last." Her tone was disapproving. Tavy saw

Harry and Louisa glance at her, then at each other, before they continued to talk. She answered the Mistress's questions — why was she so late? Where had she been? — her attention kept straying to the pair by the piano, half listening to their familiar banter, their brother-and-sisterly teasing that excluded the rest of the room. She stared at her muddy boots and tried to concentrate on what the Mistress was saying.

"You see, it is so very different from the gentle English countryside. And you are a Londoner, are you not, Octavia?"

"Yes, ma'am." The other two were listening now.

"And yet you wander alone in the bush. After twenty-two years, I would hesitate to do so. There are many unexpected dangers." She turned to the piano. "Is that not so, Harry?"

"Indeed it is, Mama, even for such country bumpkins as ourselves, eh, Louisa?"

"Country bumpkins! How dare you, Harry!" She gave him a swipe with a music book, but her show of indignation dissolved into laughter. She knew that Harry's tease was an indirect dig at Tavy. And Tavy herself had noticed it too. She clenched her fists. They were mean to mock her; they knew she could say nothing to get her own back. She wished Tom Grundy was here. He'd stick up for her. Or her good friend Duggan . . . But the Mistress was still speaking to her.

". . . just outside the Tallangatta boundary on the other side of the creek, a rough type of bushman, so Harry tells me, with no licence for that run of land. It is exceedingly unfortunate that he should have chosen to come so close to the homestead and it would be imprudent for you to venture beyond the orchard. Do you understand, Octavia?"

"Yes, ma'am." Tavy went on staring at her boots. So Jake had been mentioned at last.

The Mistress rose from her chair.

"That is settled then. Now I have a little surprise for you."

Tavy looked up. A surprise? The Mistress was smiling. "Come with me." She led the way along the passage to a room next to the side door. It was known as the nursery, although the cot and toys had long since been pushed to one side for now the Mistress used it as her workroom. On the table were lengths of cloth, scissors, needles, embroidery silks. A dressmaker's dummy was draped in pink muslin, untrimmed bonnets sat rakishly on hat stands and the old rocking horse in the corner wore measuring tapes, ribbons and braid round his neck.

"Now, let me see," the Mistress said, opening a large wicker basket and taking out an armful of clothes. There was a smell of camphor and lavender that reminded Tavy of the linen cupboard at Saint Agatha's. She watched the Mistress shake out one of the garments, a dress of blue sprigged cotton with a small lace collar. She laid it over the back of a chair and held up another of green and white striped dimity. There was a pink one next, prettier still, patterned with tiny brown and white flowers.

"I think these should fit you," she said, holding the pink one up against Tavy. "Slip off your dress and try it on."

Tavy gaped at her. "But ma'am, they're lovely. I mean . . . "

"Do as I say, Octavia," the Mistress chided her gently. "The weather will be growing warmer soon. You will need cooler clothes. These launder very nicely, so you will be able to keep fresh and clean."

Tavy's hands trembled, her cheeks burned as she fumbled with the tiny buttons.

"There now," said the Mistress, studying her with her head on one side. "Turn round. Yes, it is a trifle loose. I hope, however, you will soon become a little fatter." She smiled. "Mrs. O'Rourke tells me she is doing her best."

Tavy looked down at the dress, holding out the folds of the skirt.

"But I couldn't possibly wear these for working in, ma'am."

"Why ever not? With the aprons I provided for you, they will be quite suitable. Look at yourself in the glass." She turned the mirror towards Tavy. "Now do you not consider it most becoming?"

Tavy stared at her reflection. "Oh ma'am," she said at last, turning to the Mistress with shining eyes, "it's ever so pretty." She wanted to throw her arms round her neck and hug her.

"Excellent. Then you are happy and these little dresses will be put to good use. Louisa grew so rapidly that she scarcely wore them."

Louisa? Tavy's elation popped like a bubble. "But Miss Louisa won't like me to wear her clothes, ma'am," she said, anxiously.

"Nonsense, Octavia. They are no use to her now. I have told her already that I intend them for you. I wish you to wear them. You understand?"

"Very good, ma'am," Tavy answered in a subdued voice. All her delight in the dresses had vanished. She could imagine how Louisa would dislike to see a servant wearing her pretty clothes, even though she had long since outgrown them. But what could she do? The Mistress was quite adamant. She would have to suffer Louisa's sneers.

The Mistress was rearranging the contents of the basket. She held up a tiny lace bonnet.

"These baby things," she sighed. "So many years ago, such happy days." She put back the bonnet and turned to Tavy with a smile. "I had such darling babies."

Tavy nodded, thinking of Joe. "I love babies," she said, with a sudden longing to see him.

"You cared for them in England?" the Mistress asked, surprised at the fervour in Tavy's voice.

"No, ma'am. I never did. But, well, I just do love them."

"Perhaps one day you will have one of your own," the Mistress said, opening the door.

"I hope so, ma'am," Tavy said. But it's Joe I want, she added to herself, gathering up the dresses. And not you nor anybody else in the world is going to stop me seeing him again.

All the same, for the next few days Tavy decided it would be wiser not to go to the hut. There would be trouble if she

71

was caught going through the paddocks. It was that stockman, Sam, who always seemed to be watching her. 'Old Stickybeak', Lily called him.

"He never says much except when he's tipsy," she told Tavy. "He was one of them prisoners what was sent out from England as a punishment and he's been sour about it ever since. He's worked for the Campions for ever so long and they've been real good to him. He'll do anything for Master Harry 'cos he's known him since he was a littl'un. Mind you, Master Harry thinks a lot of Sam too, reckons Sam's the best stockman round these parts. And as for knowing what's going on, he never misses a thing, Sam don't."

Well, I don't want him telling tales on me, Tavy thought, and she comforted herself that Jake would be unlikely to go hunting again for a while, so she would not be able to see Joe anyhow.

Reluctantly, she wore Louisa's old dresses, the blue one first because it was the plainest. As she had expected, Louisa gave her a look of cold disdain, sniffing and pursing her lips when the Mistress nodded approvingly and said, "Very nice, Octavia." She noticed Harry raise his eyebrows and stare at her with a cynical half smile as she helped Lily to serve the supper that evening.

"It's a lucky girl, you are," Mrs. O'Rourke told her. "Suits you a treat, doesn't it, Lily?"

Lily did not answer and Tavy guessed that she was jealous.

"The Mistress never gave me no dresses," she said later, when they were in their room. She picked up the green and white dimity and held it against her. "Trouble is, I'm too bulgy." She climbed on the chair and studied herself sideview in the small mirror. "Look at that!" She patted her stomach and laughed. "Oh well, there's some as likes me this way. And," she winked at Tavy, "it's my half day tomorrow."

On Sunday morning, the Master conducted family prayers in the drawing room. Tavy stood at the back with

Mrs. O'Rourke and Lily, while Louisa, frowning at the music, played 'All people that on earth do dwell' very slowly, with frequent mistakes. And a funny lot of people they are, Tavy thought, listening to the different voices round her: Lily letting herself go in a loud contralto, Mrs. O'Rourke droning on one note, and the Master, who faced them in his wheel chair, gazing straight ahead, his deep voice always a fraction behind the piano. The Mistress sang slightly tremolo, glancing affectionately at her dearest Harry, who stood next to her holding his hymnal at arm's length, conscious of his tuneful baritone. After the hymn, with much grunting and heavy breathing from Mrs. O'Rourke, they knelt for the prayers — and such long prayers. Would they ever end, Tavy wondered, peeping through her fingers.

Sun filtered through the thick net curtains, warming the small stuffy room. She longed to escape into the fresh air. The feeling made her think of the lower deck of the *Henrietta*, of Joe in his box in the dark hut. He should be outside. "Little ones should have plenty of fresh air," Aunt Lavender always said. "It brings roses to their cheeks." But there would be no chance to take Joe out today because Lily was having the afternoon off. It was clear that Lily did not intend to waste a moment of it. Swallowing the last of her baked jam roll, she dumped her plate in the sink and, pausing at the door to call, "Tootle-oo, my lovelies", she disappeared.

When Tavy had washed up, it was almost time to start preparing the tea trays. She would just have time to run outside and look round the garden before Mrs. O'Rourke woke up. As she came round the corner of the house, she caught sight of Louisa and her mother sitting in the shade of the casuarina tree. She turned and ran to the far gate that led into the orchard, keeping well away from the sheep pens in case Sam was there. It was the first time she had gone beyond the apple trees and she was surprised to find that the orchard stretched along the whole length of the paddocks. She walked through groves of cherries, pears and plums, recognising the tiny green fruit among the leaves. Fancy having all this in your back garden, she thought, and when, further on, she saw ripe lemons and oranges, she stared in amazement. There was a whole fruit salad! She laughed out loud and thought of Tom Grundy. He would think that was funny too. She wandered down towards the paddocks and leaned over the fence to watch the lambs. Ever so pretty you are, she told them; just like toys. I wish I could take one of you for poor little Joe. He hasn't got any toys. She looked over at the dense trees, longing to see him again. But, after the Mistress's warning, she would have to be careful not to be seen going in that direction. Then she noticed that there was a hedge running along the edge of the last paddock. If she climbed the fence at the end of the orchard, she could slip down the far side of the hedge and reach the wood without even Sam knowing where she had gone. She ran back happily singing to herself 'Bye baby bunting, Jake's gone a-hunting'. Perhaps tomorrow he would.

She had forgotten that Monday was wash day. The sun shone, the wind was brisk and in a few hours the laundry was ready to iron. "Fair shares this time," Tavy said to Lily, dividing the linen between them. Lily scowled and grumbled. Her half day seemed to have tired her out. But Tavy was firm and, although she too had to gopher and crimp, she finished in time to go down to the hut. Don't let Jake be there, don't let Jake be there. The words went round in her head as she ran along the far side of the hedge, down to the creek, across the stepping stones and on to the edge of the trees.

"Oh no!" she whispered. The horse was there, grazing under the trees. All the same, she went on cautiously towards the hut, with the faint hope that Jake might have gone somewhere on foot, taking the dog with him. But before she had gone more than a few steps, she heard the thwack of his axe and, peering round the corner, she saw him felling trees at the edge of the clearing. He wouldn't notice if she darted in and saw Joe for a moment.

But the dog was lying near the door. She hated that dog; it was ugly and vicious and it was the only thing that was keeping her from Joe. She had a sudden urge to knock it on the head and silence it, though she knew that she could never do anything so cruel. After all, it was a good watchdog, protecting Joe. She watched it gnawing at its parched bone. Perhaps, if she made friends with it — but how? And she turned away and walked slowly back.

It was the next day, when she was helping Lily to clear away the dinner plates, that Tavy had an idea about the dog.

"Pernickety, aren't they?" Lily remarked, scraping the remaining lamb chops into the waste bin. "They've barely eaten half of these."

To start with, Tavy had been shocked by such extravagance. 'Waste not, want not', Aunt Lavender had taught and, at Cadogan Square, Cook had always saved the end of the joint for mince or stew. Now she had learned that here all leftovers were thrown away. Even Bron, the old sheepdog, sniffed at anything but his own favourite cuts of meat. "He doesn't like scraps," Mrs. O'Rourke said. But it suddenly occurred to Tavy that there was another dog that did.

The rubbish bins stood outside the kitchen door, beside piles of old newspapers. When the dishes were finished, it took Tavy a few seconds to retrieve the chops, wrap them in newspaper and, hiding them under her apron, to run into the orchard. She almost hoped that Jake would have left the dog behind today. It would be disappointing not to be able to try out her plan. Breathlessly, she ran to the edge of the trees. It was all just as the day before, the horse in the clearing, Jake cutting wood and the dog . . . she looked round the corner of the hut. Yes, the dog was still worrying the same old bone. She threw the chops at it, one by one, edging slowly forward, telling it that it was a good dog, that she was its friend and did it want another nice bit of meat, until she reached the door and slipped inside.

"Joe, sweetest Joe!" She picked him up and hugged him. It seemed so long since she had seen him, four whole days. She was sure he had grown. But he did look pale. "You should be outside in the fresh air," she told him. "When your Dada goes hunting, I'll take you for a walk."

The next day, Jake did go out with his horse and the dog. She had to throw the meat scraps into the bushes, but what did that matter? She had the whole afternoon alone with Joe. She moved his box out into the sunshine, while she cleaned the hut and washed the dirty clothes. Somehow, here it did not seem like work. Was it because she was independent, because nobody was giving her orders? Or was it the peacefulness of this place that gave her a feeling of freedom and space? Of course Tallangatta was just as remote; it was a beautiful homestead, the Mistress was kind, but she was strictly a servant obeying orders and what was the use of wages when there was nothing to spend them on? In London, she had taken it for granted, grateful that she had a position in such a fine house, even though she was only a scullery maid earning ten shillings a month. She tried to talk about this feeling to Lily, when they were doing the housework.

"Find yourself a man then," Lily said, shaking the duster out of the window. "That's what I'm going to do. Someone with thousands and thousands of sheep who'll make a fortune and . . ."

"Like Harry?" Tavy interrupted her.

Lily swung round, blushing. "Whatever gave you that idea?"

"He's got thousands of sheep — well, his father has — and miles of land."

Lily shrugged. "I might rather live in the town, somewhere big like Sydney. There's not many fine houses in Gunderra, where I grew up. I'll have a mansion with servants of my own, never do a stroke of work."

"Oh, it's not work I mind," Tavy said, "and I wouldn't want to be in a town. I like it in the country where there's space — that's what I like." She stretched her arms sideways.

"Space all round me."

Lily grinned. "Trying to be a bird?" She copied Tavy, flapping round the room like a huge cockatoo.

Tavy burst out laughing. She picked up the mop and chased Lily, till they both collided into the wash stand and stopped abruptly, listening for the Mistress's footsteps. After that, Tavy's urge to be a bird became a joke between them. It was a convenient explanation for Lily's inquiries as to where she disappeared to in the afternoons, for now she went to the hut as often as she could. There were often days when she could not go, when there was ironing to be done, butter to be churned in the dairy — a new task to Tavy, which she found tedious and slow — vegetables to be picked and weeds to be hoed in the kitchen garden for, though Garrity, the groom, was also the gardener, most of his time was spent with the horses. Lily hated weeding. "Dirty, back-breaking work," she grumbled and, though Tavy liked being outside in the sunshine, she resented anything that kept her from Joe.

She thought about him constantly, especially when two or three days passed without seeing him, worrying that Jake left him alone so much. Joe was getting much stronger now. He could sit up on his own and he kicked vigorously, rocking his box. Supposing he tipped it over and was trapped underneath; supposing some strange bushman came to the hut when Jake was out with the dog. Increasingly, she hated to leave him, but she was careful never to stay for long, particularly if Jake was in the clearing. She was constantly aware that any moment he might come back, though as time went by she grew less concerned. He seemed to work steadily for several hours, felling trees, digging, and now he was driving in stakes round the edge of the clearing. Sometimes she was so absorbed in caring for Joe that she forgot about Jake altogether. Then she would remember and say to Joe, "What shall I do if I hear your Dada coming? Where can I hide? Under the blankets on the bed? He might sit on me! And the little back window is too small to climb through. I might get stuck." She laughed and Joe smiled back at her, showing his two new teeth. No, she would just have to face Jake and hope he would not be angry with her for intruding. He might even be pleased that she had cleaned the hut — if he had noticed! At least he must have noticed the pile of new bones outside. Even after a day's hunting, when the dog had been given an enormous raw joint, it seemed just as greedy for the scraps Tavy brought. She disliked it less now; in fact, when it pricked up its ears and wagged its tail at her, she felt almost brave enough to pat it. Almost, but not quite. She called it Wolf, because it looked like a wolf and giving it a name made it more of a friend. There were always leftovers from dinner to bring and it wasn't dishonest, she assured herself, because although the household waste was taken to the farm for the poultry, she reckoned that the hens could spare a bone or two for Wolf. She collected them quickly on her way to the orchard and, by keeping to the far side of the hedge at the end of the paddocks, she was confident that Sam could not see her.

The undergrowth was dry now and each time she went down to the creek she found her track easier to follow. She was no longer startled by the cries and sudden flight of birds, and once she caught sight of a kangaroo disappearing into the bush. Lily had said that they were pests because they ate all the grass, but Tavy thought them beautiful creatures. Sometimes they came at dusk out on the plain behind the farm. If there was time before she helped Lily to serve the supper, she would slip out and watch them, still as statues, almost indistinguishable from the grey-brown trunks of the gum trees. Then, as if at some secret signal, they would spring away with long, lithe leaps, till they were lost in the dwindling light. The sky was at its most mysterious then, luminous, endless as time and, if she stared up for long enough, she would see the first star, a pin point of light.

Chapter Seven

It had been the best afternoon of all. Jake had gone out with Wolf and his horse. There was nobody there except for the goat grazing peacefully behind the privy. And Joe. Joe was at his most endearing; playful and happy and oh, she did love him. When she had washed the clothes, tidied Jake's bed and swept the floor, she took him for a walk round the clearing, pointing out the flowers, the trees, the birds, "and look at all the digging your Dada's done and the nice strong stakes he's been putting in". Then they sat on the grass outside the hut. Joe enjoyed his freedom, kicking and rolling onto his front. He even managed to shunt himself backwards with a bouncy rocking motion that made Tavy laugh. He was cutting two more teeth and everything he could grasp was stuffed into his mouth. She gave him a crust of damper to chew then, after a drink of milk, he grew drowsy so she carried him inside and tucked him into his box. The sun was still high. There would be time to collect the washing before Jake came back; she would bring in some firewood too, she thought. That would be a help.

She tiptoed to the door, then stopped abruptly, one hand on the latch. There was a man in a cabbage tree hat on the far side of the clearing. Jake! She dodged back behind the door, peering through the crack. No, it wasn't Jake. This man was older, skinnier, somehow familiar. Then he turned and she saw his face. It was Sam. Why was he here? She watched him going slowly from stake to stake, pushing them as if to test how firm they were. He crossed to the patch of newly dug ground and stood with his thumbs in his belt, digging the toe of his boot into the soil. Then, with a glance all round as if to see if anyone was watching, he started to walk towards the hut. Tavy drew a sharp breath. Quick! She must hide! In a panic she stared round the small bare room, though she knew there was only one possible place: Jake's bed. Rumpling the neatly folded covers into a heap, she burrowed underneath, pulling them right over her head. Then she lay rigid, hardly daring to breathe, listening for footsteps. She could hear nothing. The heavy bedclothes muffled all sounds. They were hot and scratchy and the kangaroo skins smelled rancid and foul. What was Sam doing? Had he come to see Jake? Or was he just curious, nosing round? He had had a good look at the stakes and the patch Jake had dug. Supposing he came right into the hut? He might have come already and be standing quite close to her at this moment! She felt trickles of sweat run down her sides, her nose itched and she prayed that she wouldn't sneeze. How long had she been there? She tried to think of something else, but her mind turned to Joe and he was here too. Was he all right?

She heard a faint pattering. Then there was something touching her face, something wet and warm. She flung back the covers. Wolf! She jerked up. There was no sign of Sam. Wolf wagged his tail furiously, whining at her. Had Jake come back? And Sam, was he still outside? She sprang up, noticing that Joe was still asleep, and ran to the door. The clearing was empty. Then she heard a whistling sound coming from the trees. Not a bird, but Jake riding straight towards her. It was too late to run away, pointless to hide again under the covers. She took a deep breath and stepped outside. The whistling stopped. Jake reined in his horse and for a moment he stared at her. Then he dismounted and led his horse towards her.

"Good day," he said.

Tavy bobbed a curtsy. She didn't know why. It just happened. Perhaps it was part of the apology she wanted to make but, although she opened her mouth, no sound came out.

Jake hitched his horse to the tree stump near the door and slung the gun off his shoulder. "Heel!" he shouted at Wolf, who was still circling Tavy's skirts, and immediately the dog slunk to his side. "Lie down," Jake ordered. Wolf dropped to the ground.

"He does what you tell him!" Tavy said in surprise, suddenly finding her voice.

Jake raised his eyebrows and nodded. "Yep, 'e's all right with me, wild as a dingo with other folks," he said, tying Wolf to his rope.

"He's a good watch dog."

Jake grinned. "He's made friends with you all right."

She nodded. "I brought him bones."

"And you cleaned up inside."

Tavy nodded again. "Did you guess it was me?"

"Saw you a few times."

"You saw me!" Tavy exclaimed. "But you never . . ." she hesitated. How strange that he had not come and talked to her. "You didn't mind?"

"Mind?" He shrugged. "It's what the place needs. I got no one else to do it now."

"I came because of Joe," Tavy explained, lest he thought she was trying to take the place of his woman. "He's left on his own so much," she added.

"I'm in the clearing most times." He spoke defensively.

She nodded. That was true. If anyone came, Wolf would bark. It was only by bribing him with food that he had let her pass. "But you take him when you go hunting," she said.

"Got to train him to the gun. Besides, I can't chance leaving him. Damn dog could break his rope, get on Campion's property. Be the devil to pay if he went after their sheep."

"But supposing somebody came, a stranger. What about Joe?"

Jake looked away, his face troubled. "There's none as comes out here." He paused, kicking at a tussock of grass with his boot. "Well, damn few." Perhaps he was thinking of the traveller who went off with his woman, Tavy thought, and there was me and Sam just now. Should she tell him Sam had been here? She hesitated, then she remembered Joe all alone.

"There was a man here today, before you came back, the stockman from Tallangatta."

Jake glanced up sharply. "That old stickybeak! What's he after?"

"Don't know. He didn't see me. I was hiding." She did not tell him where. "He was looking at the stakes and the ground you dug up."

"Nosy old devil!" He jerked his head at the newly turned ground. "That's for tatties and turnips, maybe a few apple trees and such like."

"You're planning to stay here?"

"Why not?" He was on the defensive again.

Tavy did not answer. She wondered if he knew about the licence, about Harry wanting this run by the creek. She hoped he wouldn't leave. That would mean losing Joe. But Joe needed food, good nourishing food, more than just goat's milk, wild game and home grown vegetables. Jake would have to buy provisions and, though she knew he had some money in the wallet he kept slotted onto his belt, that wouldn't last for ever. He would have to earn his living somehow. She watched him undo the rope round a carcase tied to the saddle. A trail of blood dripped down the horse's flank. Wolf strained at his rope, yapping and whining.

"I'd better go now," Tavy said.

Jake glanced at her, saying nothing. She began to walk away, then stopped and looked round. "Would it be all right . . . " she started.

Jake was heaving the carcase off the horse. He threw it on the ground, out of Wolf's reach, and began to unbuckle the saddle.

Tavy tried again. "Would it be all right if I came back sometimes to see Joe and . . . ?"

"Yep." The answer was firm. "Yep," he repeated. "You keep coming."

82

Tavy suddenly felt light with happiness. She beamed at Jake.

"Oh, I will. Thank you ever so much. I'll come again soon."

"You been stretching your wings again?" Lily said, as Tavy ran breathlessly into the kitchen. She had raced back, keeping a wary eye open for Sam, but she had seen no sign of him. Mrs. O'Rourke looked up from her plate of meat pie.

"Come on, girl. We've started our tea."

So she was hardly late at all. She thought she had been lying under Jake's bedclothes for hours and hours. She sat down at the table, smoothing back her hair.

"You look like you been through a hedge backwards," Mrs. O'Rourke commented.

"I was in the orchard." Well, it was true. She went through the orchard.

"Trying to be a bird," said Lily with a giggle. "Can you fly yet?"

"Nearly," Tavy told her cheerfully.

She slipped out again when the meal was over. Lily would chatter and she wanted time to think about everything that had happened that afternoon. She had known Jake was bound to discover her eventually, but she had been afraid he might be hostile, resenting her intrusion. It was a relief to find he did not mind, that anyway he had guessed it was she who had been cleaning the hut. He had even seen her a few times and she had been so sure that she had kept out of sight! Now she could come and look after Joe without the worry of Jake returning; he could tell her which days he planned to go hunting so that she could try to be there when Wolf was not outside to guard Joe. You never knew when some stranger might appear. She wouldn't be surprised if that stickybeak Sam came nosing round again. At least she was confident that he had not known she was there. For all she knew, he might have looked through the door, but even under Jake's heavy covers she would have heard his boots if he had come inside. Wolf's footsteps were light enough and she had caught the sound of them.

She ran past the stables and on towards the farm. The sun had set and the scattered puffs of cloud were tinged with pink. She gazed out across the plain, searching for kangaroos. And there they were — three, four, half a dozen or more, motionless in the still air. She clapped her hands above her head and instantly they came alive, leaping away, further and further, till she could see them no longer. A sudden cacophony startled her, that crazy laughter in the trees. Kookaburras. She knew that now. She looked up and saw them perched on a branch. But still for a moment the noise alarmed her. It would always remind her of Willie Moser.

As she passed the stables on her way back, she heard someone talking, an indistinct mumble, then another voice, loud and strong.

". . . waste of good pasture. He could just as well dig up another run, away from our boundary, damn him."

It was Harry and he sounded angry. She went a little closer. It was the mumbler again and she could not hear his words, but she glimpsed the brim of a hat, a cabbage tree hat. It was stickybeak Sam. If he's not telling Master Harry about Jake's clearing, she thought, I'll be very, very surprised. The mumbling stopped, there was movement from within. Picking up her skirts, she turned and fled.

Tavy did not have to wait long for proof that she was right. Later, when she and Lily went to the dining room to collect the supper dishes, Harry was speaking in the same angry tone.

". . . driving in stakes as if he owned the place."

"Nothing you can do about it, son." The Master's voice was slow and firm. "It's outside our boundaries."

"But that's good grazing land, Papa. Sam says that with the new stock we'll need more pasture. He's been trying to clear the bush below the paddocks, but the grass is poor compared to the rich feed along the creek. You know I want to add that run to our property, and if we wait much longer

84

this fellow will have got a licence and will start to expand himself."

"Why not go and talk to him, Harry dear?" the Mistress suggested. She handed Tavy the potato dish. "Perhaps you could persuade him nicely to move to another run."

Harry turned to her. "I doubt he could be persuaded nicely, Mama. According to Sam, he is a rough-tongued bushman, out for what he can get."

"And so are most of the free-settlers who come here," the Master pointed out. "Sam bears a grudge against any man who commits what he considers a crime and gets away with it, when long ago he was deported for petty theft. He is loyal to us because we have treated him well, and he has always been devoted to you, Harry."

"Yes, how he loved you," the Mistress said, smiling to herself. "I remember him taking you to see the new lambs when you were just a tiny lad."

"And such a pretty little lad!" Louisa mocked, twisting away as Harry tweaked her ringlet.

"Children, please." The Mistress clicked her tongue.

Harry turned to his father again. "But seriously, Papa, could you not write to the Lands Commission and ask them to send a licence for that run?"

Louisa fiddled with her spoon. She found this conversation tedious.

"It is not the least use writing to them, Harry," the Master said firmly, leaning towards his son. "By the time the letter reaches them, the Commissioner will be here."

"But, Papa," Harry spoke impatiently. "He's not due again till the new year. By then, that slathering bodgie will have . . ."

"Harry! Such language in front of the girls!" The Mistress was shocked. She glanced anxiously at Louisa, then at Lily and Tavy, who hastily piled the last plates onto the tray. There was an ominous clatter as Lily went through the door. Tavy shut it quickly behind them.

"Oops!" Lily gasped, her face crimson. "I nearly dropped it!"

When they were outside, they dissolved into giggles.

"Slathering bodgie," Lily echoed. "Thought I'd burst!"

"You looked like you were going to," Tavy said. "Is it so dreadfully rude?"

"Bush talk, that's all," Lily told her. She pursed her lips. "But we mustn't let our precious Louisa hear such unladylike words, must we?" She pulled a face and they were off again, the plates sliding perilously on the tray.

"D'you think Master Harry meant that bushman whose woman ran off and left him?" Tavy asked, when the dishes were safely deposited on the kitchen table.

"Reckon so," Lily said. "He's the slathering bodgie." And she collapsed onto a chair in fresh gales of mirth.

Mrs. O'Rourke turned on them, bristling. "If you two don't get in there quick with this lemon syllabub, I'll lay about the pair of you with the rolling pin."

The weather grew warmer. It was November now. The cherries in the orchard would soon be ripe and there was a row of crimson tulips along the front of the homestead.

"They're ever so pretty," Tavy said when the Mistress found her admiring them. "Just like Hyde Park."

The Mistress smiled. "Do you miss it, Octavia?"

Tavy thought for a moment. "I don't really know, ma'am, but sometimes I feel, well, upside down. It's the sky, I think. It's different here."

"Everything is different here, Octavia," the Mistress said with sadness in her voice.

"Oh, not your flowers, ma'am. They look just like they do at home."

The Mistress shook her head. "Not really." She sighed. "It is my English garden I miss most of all, my smooth green lawn, my roses — and the butterflies. Here we have such nasty flies."

Tavy hated the flies. They buzzed round Joe as he slept, settling on his face. Tavy flicked them away. "Get off, nasty pests."

Jake shook his head at her. "They ain't bad yet."

She saw more of him now, although he kept away from the hut most of the time she was there. Once or twice he had muttered gruff thanks as she had left to go back to Tallangatta, but she was never sure he really liked having her around. She sensed that he felt ill at ease with her. Was he still ashamed of staring at her in her underclothes? Sometimes she noticed him watching her from his vegetable patch. At first she smiled and waved, but she soon gave up for he always turned away and started digging again. He had planted the potatoes and turnips and was preparing more ground for pumpkins and cabbage. "Joe'll be eating them soon," he told her. It was Joe who mattered.

He talked to Joe, seldom to Tavy. And Joe responded eagerly. He was always excited when Jake appeared, holding out his arms to be picked up. It was silly to be jealous, Tavy told herself. After all, Joe was his son. Joe knew him best. But when Joe sat on his lap, smiling, laughing, pulling at his beard, Tavy could not help wishing she had Joe to herself. Sometimes she took Joe outside and sat with him behind the hut where he could not see Jake, and on their walks she would keep well away from the vegetable patch. Joe was too heavy now to carry far; he could sit up on his own and was trying to crawl. His little wooden box was far too small. Tavy thought of the empty cot in the work room at Tallangatta. It would be perfect for Joe. But Jake made him a new one with deeper sides so that he could not roll out. Joe's appetite had increased as well and he drank much more milk now the weather was warm. Tavy asked Jake to show her how to milk the goat. She watched while he sat beside it, squirting jets of milk into the pail between his knees. It looked easy enough but, when she tried, the goat would not keep still. Each time she managed to grip its teats, it moved to another tuft of grass and the milk missed the pail. Once, when it was almost full, she knocked it over. Joe cried with hunger; he didn't like drinking boiled water from the creek. Tavy made him broth from bones and lean meat, skimming it carefully and seasoning it with salt. With

Jake to tend the fire, she baked the damper, mixing milk and flour, shaping it into a flat, round loaf and pushing it into the hot ashes with a long-handled shovel. The first few she made were heavy and tough. She would have liked to throw them away, but Jake's stock of flour was getting low. He ate them without comment, but Joe spat his out. It annoyed her that Jake could make better damper than she could.

"How d'you make damper?" she asked Mrs. O'Rourke.

"I don't," Mrs. O'Rourke told her bluntly. "I make bread and very good bread it is too, my girl. You'll not be catching me making that terrible damper."

"Well, I'll make it," Tavy said to herself. "I'm determined to."

At last, one Sunday, her afternoon off, she baked a beauty, crusty and light. She laid it on the table and looked at it proudly. It smelled delicious. Jake should be pleased. She would have liked to show him at once, but she was afraid he would be angry if she interrupted his work. Then she heard Wolf barking and went to the door to see what was the matter. There was a horse in the clearing, a fine chestnut, and beside it, standing with his back to her, was Harry. She shot back quickly into the shadow. Whatever happened, he must not see her. Peering through the crack in the door, she could see Jake walking slowly towards him, dragging his spade. She wished that she could hear what they were saying, but Wolf was making too much noise. It was Harry who was doing the talking, using his hand to emphasize some point, while Jake leaned on his spade, staring at the ground. Eventually, he looked up and shook his head. His reply was brief. For a moment Wolf was quiet and Tavy could hear Harry's voice, loud and impatient.

"Look here, Bushman, can't you understand there's miles of unoccupied land to the west? Why pick on this run, right on our boundary?"

Wolf started barking again, the horse became restless, tossing its head and Harry jerked at the rein. Then he began to speak again and Tavy could tell from his actions that his blood was rising. He swung out his arm, pointing round the clearing and, as he turned towards the hut, she backed away from the door. Joe was asleep in his new cot. She stared down at him, thinking. Would Jake have to move? But Harry could not make him. He had no more right to this run than Jake. She suddenly realised that Wolf had stopped barking. There was the sound of heavy boots just outside and Jake ducked through the door. Tavy looked at him anxiously. His face was grim, his mouth set in a hard line. He flung his hat onto the table and dropped onto the chair, propping his head in his hands. Leaning over, Tavy extracted the damper from underneath his hat, sliding it on the edge of the table. She went to the door and peeped out. Wolf was gnawing his bone, Jake's horse grazed in the shade, switching away the flies with its tail. Harry had gone. She turned back to Jake.

"What did he want?"

There was no reply. She went up to the table.

"What did he say to you?"

Still Jake said nothing. For a moment, she watched him. Why didn't he answer? She touched his arm.

"Please do tell me." His silence made her all the more determined to make him speak. She tried again. "See, I've baked another damper. It's better this time. It smells good, doesn't it?" She held it under his nose. "Don't you think so, Jake?"

At the sound of his name, he jerked up his head. "What d'you want, keeping on asking and asking me?" He glared at her and she stepped back, alarmed.

"I was only . . ."

"Leave me alone, see, 'tis all I want. That damned Campion, giving me orders. Just 'cos he's got money, he reckons he can get rid of me. And that stockman poking around. And you blathering on about . . ."

"Blathering on! How dare you say that!" Tavy lifted her chin, her eyes wide with anger. "I was showing you the damper. I'm sorry I made it now. It's for Joe, just Joe. I only come because of him, because you don't look after him. You

89

just leave him alone all day and . . ."

"Stop your mouth." With a violent movement, Jake lunged towards her, knocking the table. She darted back with a cry of fear. There was a clatter, a crash, as plates, mugs, tins, knives and the beautiful damper fell to the floor.

"Oh!" Tavy covered her face with her hands. She could hear Joe crying behind her but, as she turned to go to him, Jake blundered past her and lifted him out of his cot. He held Joe close, bending over him. Tavy looked at them together, their heads touching, Joe's small and round, his hair like silk, Jake's darker in colour, matted and coarse. It seemed as if Jake was protecting Joe, protecting him from her. Joe! Oh Joe! she cried in her heart and she stumbled to the table, choking with sobs. She stared down at the jumbled heap on the floor; tears ran down her face and she let them fall, tasting the salt, seeing them drop into the puddle of milk on the hard earth floor. She saw Jake go out, still clasping Joe. Then, slowly, she knelt and, sobbing aloud, she began to pick up the broken damper.

Chapter Eight

It was hard to hide her unhappiness. It was not just the memory of Jake's unexpected violence, the injustice of it, the ingratitude. It was Joe. Each time she thought about him, fresh tears pricked her eyes and she had to blink hard and rub her nose with the back of her hand. It was the way Jake had held him, not just to comfort him, but shutting her out, keeping Joe away from her. Why? Why, when she had not only looked after Joe but also had cleaned the hut, washed the nappies, and Jake's filthy clothes, milked that goat who wouldn't stand still, baked dampers — such a beautiful damper the last one had been, till Jake had knocked it off the table and ruined it. And then he'd accused her of 'blathering on at him'. Thinking of that set her crying again.

Stop it, she told herself. What did it matter if the damper was broken? It served Jake right. She was glad she hadn't picked up all that mess on the floor. She had left the bits of damper on a plate on the chair and abandoned the rest lying in the puddle of milk. It had all spilled; there had been none left for Joe. Was Jake looking after him? Oh, she had to go soon to see if he was all right. Supposing Jake took him away. Harry was trying to force Jake to move.

Although she had bathed her blotchy face as soon as she got back to Tallangatta, Lily had noticed it straight away.

"You hurt?" she asked, staring at her.

Tavy shook her head. But I am, she thought. I'm hurt inside.

"What's the matter then?"

Tavy did not answer.

"Must be something," Lily persisted.

"Leave the girl alone, Lily." Mrs. O'Rourke had patted Tavy's shoulder as she waddled past.

Lily tossed her head. "I was only asking. No harm in that."

She was scratchy. Harry had gone off round the property for several days. She spent the evenings lounging on her bed, brushing her hair.

"Chatty, aren't we?" she remarked and she sang loudly, watching Tavy out of the corner of her eye.

The Mistress had been full of sympathy. She had stopped Tavy, crossing the courtyard the next day.

"Octavia, I can see that something is troubling you. Would you like to tell me what it is?"

"No, thank you, ma'am. 'Tis nothing at all." She tried to smile.

"You are homesick, perhaps?"

Tavy had looked down without answering.

"I understand," the Mistress had said gently. "I know what it is like, my dear. The post should arrive in a week or so. Perhaps you will have a letter."

"I don't know anyone who would write to me, ma'am."

The Mistress had studied Tavy's face for a moment. "I hope you will feel that you can come and talk to me whenever you are unhappy, Octavia."

"Yes, ma'am. Thank you, ma'am," Tavy had said and she bobbed a curtsy and ran on to the kitchen.

The afternoons were the worst, the time when she usually went to see Joe. Once when the Mistress and Louisa had gone for a drive, she had slipped into the workroom and closed the door. Yes, the cot would be just right for Joe, she thought, rocking it cautiously, and there was a little bath propped against the wall, much easier than the bucket she washed him in. There were toys as well, dolls with prim china faces and real curls, a worn velvet rabbit with only one ear, the rocking horse — Joe would soon be big enough to sit on that. She had opened the wicker basket, smelling the lavender as she lifted the tissue paper and peeped at the small lace-edged garments. Then, at the thought of Joe's two shabby little shirts, a lump had come into her throat and she had closed the lid and tiptoed away.

She was glad when there was laundry to be ironed, eggs for preserving to be rubbed with wax, peas to be picked in the kitchen garden, and the early cherries were ripening now.

"Time I got on with the jam," Mrs. O'Rourke said. " 'Tis no good waiting till they're mushy. The plums'll be ready by then too and I've got the Christmas puddings and mincemeat to make. You and Lily can both get out there with baskets when you've finished the dinner dishes."

"Why can't Garrity do it?" Lily wanted to know. "He's meant to do the gardening."

"It's horses first with Garrity. You should be knowing that by now, Lily. It's never the vegetables he's caring about

92

and it's never the fruits either."

There was a continuing feud between Garrity and Mrs. O'Rourke. She could not forgive him for ignoring his Irish background. "Calls himself an Australian," she said, "and him born in the County Clare!"

The cherries were sweet and juicy, but the best always seemed to be out of reach. Tavy climbed the trees and hung her basket over a branch while Lily sat on the grass below, hooking double cherries over her ears.

"I can't stop eating them, can you, Tavy?" she called up.

"Are we allowed to?" Tavy asked, emerging from her thoughts of Joe.

"Why ever not?" Lily spat out a stone. "Nobody cares how many we eat. Most of 'em just get left to rot anyway."

Tavy popped one in her mouth. It was juicy and sweet. Joe would like these. Supposing she took some down to the hut and gave them to Jake. Would he refuse them? Of course he might eat them all himself. She would have to explain that they were for Joe as well, and remind him very politely to take out the stones in case Joe swallowed one. Perhaps he would be out. Oh, what if he were and she could have Joe all to herself! But it would only be safe to stay for a little while. If Jake returned and found her with Joe, he might become angry and violent again. He might forbid her ever to go there anymore. Just to think about it gave her a sinking feeling inside. Perhaps it would be wiser not to go; wiser possibly, but she knew all the same she could not keep away.

Tavy could hear singing, a thin, high voice quite close by her in the orchard. She stopped, peering through the trees, clutching her drawstring bag tightly in both hands. It was full of cherries, cherries for Joe. Suddenly, she caught sight of Louisa, wandering along ahead of her, carrying a basket. She dodged behind a tree trunk, her heart beating fast. She was feeling excited, but anxious too, at the prospect of confronting Jake. She had made up her mind to go today, her afternoon off, and now here was Louisa who would be bound to see her if she went on any further.

Louisa had stopped singing and was picking cherries, reaching up, her head hidden in the leaves. The moment she moved round to the far side of the tree, Tavy turned and darted back towards the sheep pens. She paused for a few seconds, to make sure Sam was not watching her, before she unlatched the gate. The first paddock was full of young rams, big, newly-shorn creatures with curly horns. She had never dared to go near them before, but they scattered vociferously as she ran down to the lower gate. The latch was stiff and she fumbled, clumsy with haste. Then suddenly it swung open and she was through, running between the trees to the creek. This side of the bush was more open now. She remembered hearing Harry say that Sam had been clearing the undergrowth to extend the paddocks. It made it easy to hurry and she was soon safely out of sight. In only a few minutes she would see the hut.

She stopped at the edge of the trees. A single grubby cloth drooped on the washing line. The goat munched steadily behind the privy and beyond in the clearing she could see Jake's horse. She gripped her bag more tightly, swallowing hard. Should she go back? No, don't be such a coward, she told herself. Go on, face him.

As she went closer, she heard Joe crying. It gave her a catch in her throat and she quickened her step, aching to comfort him. At the corner of the hut, she paused. Wolf was lying by the door. He stood up, ears pricked, watching her with yellow eyes.

"Wolf," she said softly. "Hello, Wolf."

She had forgotten to bring him any bones. He stalked towards her suspiciously.

"Wolf," she said again. He barked once, an inquiry, then louder, repeatedly. The door of the hut opened and Jake came out, looking dirtier and more dishevelled than ever. He stared at her, screwing up his eyes in the sunlight.

"Stop that," he growled at Wolf and, as the dog subsided, circling round Jake's legs, the sound of Joe's crying seemed to grow louder.

Oh, Joe! What was the matter with him? Was he ill, hungry? She remembered the cherries and held out her bag.

"I brought these for you — and Joe," she added hesitantly.

Jake looked puzzled. "What is it?"

How silly of her! He thought she was giving him the bag. She tugged at the string with trembling fingers. "Cherries." She pulled out a handful. He nodded.

"Can I put them in something? It's my bag, you see."

He picked up a tin plate, smeared with grease, lying on the ground. She regarded it doubtfully. It would make the cherries dirty for Joe, but she went up to Jake and shook them out. Her eyes moved to the open door, her face troubled. Would he mind if she went inside, just for a moment, just to see if Joe was all right? He did not seem to be annoyed with her now. She glanced at him eating cherries, spitting the stones out of the corner of his mouth.

"Long time since you been," he said.

She nodded. What could she say? Did he not realise that it was all his fault?

"Is everything all right?" she asked.

"Yep."

"Joe? Is he all right?"

"Yep."

Just that. Then why is he crying like this? Oh, tell me, please tell me. Let me see him for a minute. The words crescendoed in her head till she felt that Jake must hear them too, but he just went on eating cherries, avoiding her eye.

"Well," she said at last, "I'd best be going."

His eyebrows shot up. "You not aiming to stay?"

She looked at him with sudden hope. "You want me to?"

"If you got time."

"Oh yes!" Her eyes shone. "I'll do whatever you say, washing or sweeping, milking the goat or . . ." She hesitated. "Or Joe."

He nodded. "Like you done before," he said and, ducking under the lintel, he went inside. Tavy followed, scarcely noticing the untidiness everywhere, the flies, the stench of bad meat, as she watched Jake go to Joe's cot and pick him up. Joe's wails ceased immediately.

"Bad old boy, making that hullaballoo," Jake told him gently, patting him on the back. "Don't like being left in your cot, do you?" He glanced at Tavy. "Someone here to see you, Joe."

He turned so that Joe could see her and she went closer, holding out her finger as she had done the very first time she had come to the hut. Joe gripped it in his fist, leaning towards her, bouncing excitedly in Jake's arms.

"Joe," she whispered. He was all right after all. He needed a good wash and one crimson cheek showed that he was teething, but he was all right. For some inexplicable reason she wanted to cry.

"Reckon he's pleased to see you," Jake said. "Here, you take him. I got work to do." He dumped Joe in her arms, picked up his hat and went outside.

There was too much to be done to spend more than a moment giving Joe one rapturous hug, feeling his small, solid body — decidedly damp round the bottom — warm in her arms. Then, admonishing herself with Aunt Lavender-like briskness not to waste time, she started to clear up; Joe first, because of course he was the most important.

Having bathed him, she found that there were no clean clothes for him, no milk and only a stale end of damper. "Lucky I've brought you some cherries, Joe," she said and she was pleased to find that he liked them, smacking his lips and dribbling the juice down his chin. Then, while she was busy, she laid him on a blanket spread out on the floor where he played with a wooden spoon, banging it on a tin like a drum. She watched him kicking and rolling over, enjoying the freedom, the space around him. She knew how he felt. He was too big now to be confined in his cot. No wonder he protested when Jake left him there for hours at a time. He could almost crawl, dragging himself along on his stomach, so that she had to keep hauling him back onto his blanket. When she went round to the back to milk the goat and do the washing, she carried him with her so that she could keep an eye on him. She saw Jake watching her as she came out. Would he mind her taking Joe, think that she was trying to monopolise him? She was not sure of his reactions since his sudden outburst. To her surprise, he lifted his hand and waved, an uncertain, rather self-conscious wave. She waved back, smiling, making Joe wave too. She found that he had refilled the water buckets and, when she carried Joe back inside, she saw that the fire had been rekindled. I suppose he hopes I'll bake a damper, she thought. Well, he doesn't deserve it, but Joe will be hungry too so I'd best get on with it.

While it was cooking, she brewed tea in the billy-can, carrying it outside because the hut was hot and smoky from the fire. As she spread the blanket on the grass for Joe, she saw Jake strolling over to them.

"Could do with a wet," he said, sitting beside Joe and, when she had poured him a mug full, he gulped it down thirstily, passing it back for more.

"That's good tea, ain't it, son?" He dipped in his finger and gave Joe a lick. "Hey there, don't eat me," he added, laughing and Tavy joined in. It made everything feel easier.

"He liked the cherries," she said.

"Eaten 'em all, have you, Joe? Could do with some tucker. I'm real hungry."

Tavy fetched the rest and they shared them, stoning one or two for Joe and competing as to who could spit the pips the furthest. Jake won easily but "You're a fair spitter for a girl," he told her, avoiding her eye, and she felt warm with happiness because she understood. It was his way of telling her that he was glad she had come back, that he was sorry for what had happened last time.

She suddenly remembered the damper and, dashing inside, she pulled it out of the ashes. To her dismay, she found that it was overcooked, the crust dark and hard. She had wanted it to be specially good. Somehow it would have helped make things right again and Jake had said he was hungry. All the same, she took it out with a lump of dry cheese, apologising that she had baked it too long.

"Just how we likes it, ain't it, son?" Jake said, tearing off a hunk and eating it at once, steaming hot.

Tavy passed him the cheese. "I couldn't find any jam," she said.

"All finished. Getting low on most everything."

"Will you go to Burrawong Creek for more provisions?" She knew that Garrity drove there monthly for the Campions.

Jake shrugged. "Maybe," he muttered.

Perhaps he was worried about leaving Joe. She knew it took Garrity a whole day, driving the cart at a fast pace. Should she offer to come in the afternoon and look after Joe?

Before she could say anything, Jake stood up. "Back to work," he said, but he stayed where he was, hitching his trousers, scratching his head and jamming on his hat. He wants to say something, she thought, collecting the mugs and billy-can, prising one of Wolf's old bones from Joe's grasp.

"That's dirty," she said, giving him a spoon before he could protest.

"Behaving himself today," Jake commented. "Kicks up the devil of a fuss most times I take something away."

She picked up Joe, smiling at Jake. "He's a big boy now."

He nodded. " 'S right." He hesitated. "Fact is, I don't like leaving him on his own an', well, I'm right out of meat so I thought if you'd come an' keep an eye on him while I take the dog hunting, then . . ."

Tavy bent over Joe, concealing her delight.

"When were you thinking of?" she asked, trying to sound offhand.

"Tomorrow. Got to eat something."

"Yes," she said, adding, "I can't just come any time, you know, but I expect it'll be all right tomorrow."

"Bye, baby bunting, your Dada's going hunting," she sang to the sleepy Joe as she tucked him into his cot, and she went on singing as she cleared up the dishes and carried them out to wash. Then all at once she stopped. The goat had wandered right up to the trees. It must have broken its rope, she thought, putting down the mugs and starting towards it. But then she saw that it was not a goat at all. Its coat was stark white and it had horns. It was a sheep, newly shorn. She raced back into the clearing, calling to Jake.

"There's a sheep behind the hut. Quick, come and see."

He dropped his hoe at once and came over to her. "Sure it's not the goat?"

"No, the goat's there too, tied up behind the privy."

Wolf stood up, sensing excitement, ears pricked, a whine in his throat.

"Sit down, damn ya," Jake growled at him, turning and striding off to the back. Tavy followed, almost colliding with him as she rounded the corner. He had stopped, rigid, staring.

"What the devil!"

"Oh!" Tavy gasped. "There are lots here now!"

Four, five, no seven sheep gazed at them stupidly, chewing with a quick sideways movement.

"They're Campion's," Jake muttered. "Young rams. How the devil did they get out?"

The moment he said it, Tavy realised. These were the sheep from the paddock. She watched him walk forward, a cold fear growing inside her. The lower gate; surely she had closed it. Yet she had been in a hurry, the latch had been stiff. Jake was coming back. Should she confess? But she wasn't certain; somebody else might have left it open, there could be a hole in the fence.

"Puzzles me how they got through the bush," Jake said. "Real thick up there."

Tavy looked at him anxiously. "No," she said. "Not now. The stockman's been clearing it. I saw it when . . ."

She stopped, guiltily, afraid to go on. But Jake was not listening.

"No way I can get them back on my own," he muttered.

"I'll help you," she offered eagerly. She would do anything to make amends.

"Needs a man what knows how. You run back 'n tell that damn stockman to get down here quick."

"But . . ."

"Go on," Jake urged.

She stared at him, wide-eyed with alarm. Tell Sam! Then he would know she had been here. He would most likely blame her for leaving the gate open. He would certainly report her to Master Harry.

Jake was frowning at her. "Look, I can't keep 'em here on my own for long. If they go near the dog, there'll be real trouble. Get on with it, girl."

She gave him a last desperate glance, then she scuttled along the path to the creek.

It had seemed a very long evening. Harry had gone to Gunderra to negotiate wool sales and Lily was bored.

"Let's go watch the men play dice in the woolshed, Tavy," she had said when the supper dishes were finished. Tavy had stared at her blankly, her mind reeling with guilty fears.

"Garrity always has a game with the shepherds when they come in from the property. They're all here for the shearing. They tell some good yarns when they get a bit tipsy, specially old Sam, if he's there too. You'd be surprised how he prattles when he gets at the drink." She giggled. "Might give us a drop."

"No!" Tavy had cried out. "No, Lily, no." Not Sam and the shepherds, not after what had happened.

"Prude!" Lily had scoffed, flouncing off, leaving Tavy alone in the room.

She would have liked to go out, to watch the sky; there was comfort in its vastness, the remoteness of the stars, but she had been frightened of meeting someone. When at last Lily had come back, bumping about, singing loudly, she

100

had lain facing the wall, her eyes tight shut. Not until she heard Lily's steady breathing had she tiptoed out into the cool darkness. She had crept, barefoot, across the courtyard to the garden. Only the study window still glowed with light. She knew that the Master often read till after midnight. "His injury still pains him," she had heard the Mistress say. But he would never see her, hidden in the shadows, wrapped in her shawl.

The night air was full of the scent of flowers and the croak of tree-frogs over by the water holes came clearly through the stillness. She had heard them by the creek as she came back from that hut. The memory of it all flicked through her head like pictures in a book. Sheep, yet more sheep, bleating noisily, blundering towards her as she scrambled up the slope. She had heard a shout and ducked behind a bush. There were heavy footsteps pounding nearer, another voice shouting, an answering call. Peering round the bush, she had seen one of the shepherds and she had caught sight of Sam further off through the trees, sheep dogs too, sharp-nosed, clever. If they had sniffed her out, there would have been no escape. She had curled up small close to the ground. It was hot and prickly, flies buzzed round her head, but she stayed, not daring to move until the sounds had grown faint and she knew the men and dogs had reached the hut.

Chapter Nine

"Monday. Ugh." Lily tugged her dress over her head.

"Monday!" Tavy sat up in bed, suddenly awake. It had been growing light before she had fallen into a restless sleep. "Oh, not Monday. It can't be."

"You should know. It was your afternoon off yesterday." Lily yawned, straining the buttons on her tight dress. "Oh well, we had some fun in the woolshed last night. You ought to have come."

"What?" Tavy searched for a stocking under her bed. How could she possibly have forgotten that it was Monday? There would be ironing to do this afternoon, and she had promised Jake that she would look after Joe while he went hunting. She could not let him down after all the trouble she had caused with the sheep. Besides, she had made up her mind to tell him what had happened. Last night in the garden, she had faced the fact that she must have been the one who had left the gate unlatched. Who else could have done it? Louisa would never dare go into the paddocks, nor would the Mistress. Mrs. O'Rourke had been asleep, and certainly none of the men would forget a thing like that. She had not told anyone, even though Jake had asked her to. There had been no need. But would she have dared to if she had not seen that Sam and the shepherds were already on their way down to round up the sheep?

"They all got out," Lily was saying. "Took the men hours to get them back again. Seems that bushman's got some dingo dog tied up by his hut what went mad, barking and scaring the sheep."

"Wolf," Tavy said, shocked into awareness by Lily's words.

"No, a dog, silly, not a wolf. You never listen. What's the matter with you, Tavy? It would have woken you up hearing the names they was calling that bushman last night. Slathering bodgie." She giggled. "That weren't nothing, I can tell you. Seems he and Sam had a proper old up and downer. And I'll wager Master Harry won't be too pleased about those rams getting out when he hears tell of it. He should be home soon," she added, smiling at herself in the mirror.

By the middle of the morning, the sun had disappeared. Dark clouds moved steadily across the sky.

"Looks like we'll have to fetch all that washing in again," Lily said, shaking the mop out of the dining room window.

Tavy stuck her hand out. "Not yet," she said, though she could feel drops of rain. She wanted to make sure that the washing was too wet to iron that afternoon.

She need not have worried. Before long, there was a downpour, straight threads of water falling from the sky, drumming on the roof, drenching Lily and Tavy as they unpegged the sodden washing.

"Just our luck," Lily grumbled.

"No ironing today," Tavy said, trying not to sound too pleased.

"We need this rain badly," the Master said at dinner time. "I understand the water holes are getting low."

"And it is a joy for my garden," the Mistress added.

"But I am bored indoors all day, Mama," Louisa complained. "I wish it would stop."

It did not stop, though in the afternoon it lessened to a fine drizzle. Jake will be able to go hunting in this all right, Tavy thought, as she slithered down to the creek. She did not want him there all the time, although she hoped he would not have gone out already. She dreaded telling him it was her fault the sheep had strayed, particularly after hearing Lily's account of retrieving them. It would be better to tell him at once, get it over. Oh, she did hope that he would not be angry with her again. However, as soon as she came out of the trees, she saw that the clearing was empty, no horse, no Wolf, only the goat munching wet grass, and a pair of black and white magpies who took off with a squawk as she approached.

Joe raised his head as she went into the hut. "Dada," he said.

She went over and picked him up. "Dada's gone a-hunting, Joe," she said.

Even with Joe demanding her attention, she felt anxious, listening for the sound of Jake's return, although she knew he was unlikely to be back for a while. At first she kept the door ajar so that she could hear more easily, but the rain blew in and it was draughty for Joe playing on the floor. She sang to him as she worked, trying to forget her uneasiness.

"Bye baby bunting, Dada's gone a-hunting, he's gone to fetch a rabbit skin to wrap a baby bunting in. And you'll need a rabbit skin soon, won't you, Joe? That little shirt is far too tight and it's all worn out, but there aren't any rabbits here and you wouldn't like wearing one of those smelly kangaroo skins."

She thought of the basket full of baby clothes in the workroom at Tallangatta and she wished she could dress him in some of those. "Oh, but they wouldn't do at all for a boy like you, Joe," she told him, picking him up and looking at his small grubby face. "I'd have to spend the whole time washing them." And she laughed and danced him round the hut, singing 'Dance to your Daddy, my little Laddie' until she was suddenly startled by a sound outside. There were horse's hoofs thudding on the wet ground, the jangle of a bridle. Jake was back early. Now she would have to tell him about the gate.

She stood holding Joe, with her chin up ready to face him, as the footsteps came closer. Then, there was a loud knock on the door. Her heart bumped fast. It couldn't be Jake. There was another knock and a call.

"Bushman, are you there?"

She knew that voice. It was Master Harry. Supposing he opened the door and looked in. She stood still, with Joe in her arms, praying that he would not make a sound. He watched her with wide dark eyes. At last she heard the footsteps again, the creak of the saddle, then hoof beats growing fainter as they pounded away. After a moment, she unlatched the door and, still holding Joe, she looked out at the dripping trees. The rain had stopped, the wind was blowing the clouds apart and the birds had broken into song.

"Oh Joe," she said, taking deep breaths of fresh, cool air. "Wouldn't it have been awful if he had found us?"

"Dada," Joe said. It was his only word.

"No, Master Harry," Tavy corrected him. But Joe was right for, running towards them through the trees, was Wolf with Jake on his horse trotting briskly behind. Tavy watched him dismount and come over to them.

"How's everything?" he asked, making a grab for Wolf and tying him up. "Joe all right?"

"Oh yes," Tavy said. "He's been ever so good." She watched Jake's face, trying to gauge his mood as he tipped back his hat and gave Joe's hand an affectionate squeeze.

"Had a spot of luck today," he said. "Got a fine young 'roo. Keep us in meat for a while, Joe." He was clearly pleased with his day's hunting.

"Shall I make you some tea?" Tavy offered, wishing she had thought of it before.

"Yep. I'm dry as a bone. Not like the weather." He grinned at his own wit and Tavy nodded and smiled. Then, as he turned back to unsaddle his horse, she bustled back inside to revive the fire. By the time he came in, the billy can was almost boiling. He tossed his hat onto the table, kicked off his boots and, scooping Joe up from the floor with one hand, he sat down. Tavy hung his hat on a nail and placed his boots side by side near the hearth.

"You must have got dreadfully wet," she said solicitously.

"Could do with any amount of wet," he said. "Fills up the

105

creek. Vegetables need it too — what's left of 'em after those damned sheep trampled all over 'em."

Tavy took the billy can off the fire and carried it to the table. Now was her chance to tell him about the gate. She poured out the tea, searching for the right words.

"I, er — I didn't tell the stockman as it happened, Jake, because I saw him on his way down."

"Yep. Brought his mates, dogs, the whole lot. 'E was chasing and yelling like as if he owned the place. Can't say I care for that stockman of yours."

Tavy's eyes flashed indignantly. "He's not my stockman! He's the Campions'."

Jake blew on his tea and took a gulp. "Well, 'e don't like my dog and 'e don't like me, that's certain. Made out I were trying to pinch them rams." He snorted. "If I was aiming to pinch sheep. I wouldn't take 'em from right next door, would I? Anyways, thieving's not my game. Don't believe in it, do we, Joe?" He ruffled Joe's hair. "As for sneaking up and opening the paddock gate . . ."

"You!" Tavy gaped at him. "He said you opened it?" And she thought that Sam suspected her!

Jake grinned at her. "Don't worry, girl. It weren't really me what done it."

Tavy felt herself blush. "No," she admitted in a small voice. "It was me."

Jake took a swig of tea. "Guessed it might be," he said casually.

She stared at him aghast. "You guessed! But how?"

"Well, there ain't no one else what comes down here and you was in a bit of a state over it."

"Oh, Jake!" She clasped her hands to her head.

"No need to get in a state now. I won't split on you, girl." He lifted Joe above his head. "We wouldn't do a thing like that, would we, Joe?"

Tavy looked up at him gratefully. "I'm ever so glad you aren't angry with me. I mean, I did make a lot of trouble and Sam saying you'd let the sheep out on purpose and everything. Oh, I nearly forgot to tell you, Master Harry came while you were out. He banged on the door, but I didn't answer. I'd have been in trouble if he'd found me. The Campions don't like me coming here, you see."

Jake shrugged. "Campions don't like me at all. I know all about that." He held out his mug to be refilled. "But Joe and me likes having you all right, don't we, son? Make a good brew of tea, good damper too. Any of that left? I need some tucker."

"Master Harry's back."

Lily was radiant. She had washed her hair with rain water and it fluffed out from under her cap like wattle flowers in full bloom.

"I know," Tavy said, dragging a comb through her own mousy strands.

"How?"

"What?"

"How d'you know about Master Harry? He only got back just after dinner."

"Oh, I just passed him walking by," she said airily.

Lily glanced at her knowingly. "While you was out stretching your wings, I suppose."

"That's right," Tavy said. "I was up in the clouds."

It's true, she thought. I did fly back right up the hill with the sun through the trees and the birds gone mad and the wind showering rain all over my head.

Tavy was happy. She ran everywhere, light as a balloon. She smiled at Louisa, at Harry, she even smiled at Sam, though he doesn't deserve it, she thought, accusing Jake of trying to steal sheep. At least he did not suspect her of leaving the gate open. In fact, in spite of his watchful eye, he did not seem to have discovered her new route down to the hut. Just to make sure, she made a point of letting herself be seen around Tallangatta in the afternoons. The plums and apricots had ripened in the warm weather, driving Mrs.

107

O'Rourke into another spate of preserving. Lily and Tavy were ordered out to pick, and as before Lily lay under the trees, eating, while Tavy climbed up into the branches.

"Come and help, lazy pig," she called, dropping fruit onto Lily, and they laughed so much that Sam came over from the sheep pens to see what the noise was about.

"There's a bird up this tree," Lily told him, and he craned his neck trying to see up Tavy's skirts.

"Dirty old man," she said later, remembering Willie Moser.

"They're all as bad," Lily said with a giggle.

"Don't know what's got into you two," Mrs. O'Rourke remarked when they carried in the baskets of fruit. "Must be the warm weather." She mopped her crimson face.

"That's what it is," Lily agreed. "Sun's gone to our heads, hasn't it, Tavy?" She shook her hair and her cap flew off.

Tavy picked it up. "Moonstruck, more like," she said, tossing it back.

It was not the weather that had affected Lily. It was Harry. She disappeared each evening now and Tavy seldom heard her creep back. She noticed how carefully Harry avoided looking at Lily in front of the rest of the family, concentrating his attention on his mother to whom he was affectionate and charming, and on Louisa who encouraged his teasing. Usually he simply ignored Tavy, although once she felt his eyes on her as she waited at table.

"Cocky little thing, in spite of her looks," she heard him say as she carried out the tray.

"Ever since Mama gave her my old dresses," Louisa said. "She thinks the world of herself now."

Furiously Tavy turned and stuck her tongue out behind the door. She would have liked to wring Louisa's neck. As for that Master Harry, calling her 'cocky'; what about him? The only person who seemed to have any real authority over him was the Master and, although they discussed everything to do with the running of the property it was still the Master who made the decisions.

It was the morning after Harry came back from the wool

sales at Gunderra that Tavy heard his voice coming from the study. She had been sent to brush the passage runner, and she crawled quietly along on her hands and knees until she was a few feet from the half open door.

". . . intended to have it out with him but the place was empty," Harry was saying. "Sam suspects the gate was unlatched deliberately, Papa."

"Sam is a malicious old gossip." The Master's voice was deep and firm. "He has a grudge against the bushman and he knows you want to be rid of him so that we can acquire that run. Sam will say and do anything to curry favour."

"Sam's a good man, the best sheep-handler we have."

"That's as may be. All the same, it doesn't affect the fact that, however much of a rogue the bushman is, he would never steal those top breeding rams from right under our noses."

"There's nowhere else to steal from round here. Besides, how else did the gate come open?"

"Gust of wind, faulty catch, a gap in the fence, perhaps. Sheep are perpetually getting out. You know that as well as I do, Harry. Better have those rams moved to the paddock behind the woolshed and tell Sam to put a new latch on the gate so that it won't blow open."

"If it was the wind."

"Harry, you have absolutely no proof that it was the bushman and nor has Sam."

"True, but I shall tell Sam to keep an eye on him in future, particularly with that dog of his."

"Very well, Harry, but without aggravating the situation. That will not help matters. By all means warn him to keep his dog under control. We can't afford to lose any of the stock."

"I most certainly shall. You know, Papa, those rams are about the best we have produced. The wool samples I took to Gunderra were rated as top quality. We should get a good price this season."

"Pass me that ledger, Harry. Yes, that one. Now, last year we sold . . ."

There was a flick of turning pages. Tavy got to her feet and tiptoed back to the end of the passage. When Harry came out of the study, she was brushing the runner with vigorous concentration.

"He came all right," Jake said. "Cocky young skite."

Tavy laughed. 'Cocky' was how Harry had described her. She removed a pebble from Joe's mouth and gave him half an apricot instead. The three of them were sitting under the trees in the clearing, sharing the fruit Tavy had gathered on her way through the orchard. It was five days since she had been to the hut, but at last Mrs. O'Rourke had enough fruit to satisfy her and there was still plenty left for the gleaning. It was the apricots Joe liked best, cramming them into his mouth and dribbling out the juice. Tavy mopped his chin and flicked away the flies.

"What did Master Harry say?" she asked Jake.

"Same old blather. Why can't I move so's he can have this run? I told him I was staying, getting a licence so he'd have to put up with me and keep his damn sheep from trampling on my vegetables. He didn't like that. Made out the dog had upset his prize rams, threatened to shoot it if it chases any of his stock."

"Shoot it! But that's cruel."

Jake shook his head. " 'Tis what's done all the same. If dogs chase sheep, then dogs get shot."

"They couldn't shoot Wolf." Tavy found she had grown quite fond of him by now.

"Wolf?" Jake grinned at her. "That what you call him?"

She nodded. "Well, I didn't know what his name was."

"Didn't have one. Wolf!" he shouted across the clearing.

The dog pricked up its ears. "Yep, that's a good name for him. Behaves like a wolf too when there's sheep around. Should have seen him with them rams; nearly went mad pulling at his rope. Reckon I'll have to get him a stronger one pretty soon."

"Where can you buy one?"

110

"Get most everything at the store in Burrawong Creek."

"You're running low on flour and sugar too, and jam, tea, salt . . ."

"I know that." The words shot out, interrupting her list. Tavy glanced at him. He was frowning, chewing a stem of grass. She retrieved Joe, who was shunting himself along on his stomach like a caterpillar. "There's a hell of a lot of stuff I need," Jake muttered. "Trouble is getting a loan to pay for it. Have to find someone to vouch for me."

"I'll vouch for you," Tavy said eagerly, though she was not at all sure what the word meant.

Jake shook his head. "Wouldn't do, girl. That store at Burrawong Creek's the only place what'll give loans, and if you don't have a licence you've got to get somebody they knows about, somebody respectable like, who'll vouch for you before they'll loan you a farthing."

"You will have a licence soon though, won't you? How much does it cost?"

"Twelve shillings for a year."

"I've got seventeen shillings and sixpence. I'll give you that. And it'll soon be pay day again and then I'll have . . ."

"No," Jake said firmly. "I'm not taking your money."

"But I don't need it. There's nothing I can spend it on."

"You earned it. And you work hard for me and Joe and I don't give you nothing."

"I like coming," Tavy insisted. "You know I do."

Jake turned towards her, his eyes on her face. She felt herself blush. He seldom looked at her directly. She picked up Joe and sat him on her lap, smoothing back his silky hair.

"You need someone to look after you, don't you, Joe? I wish . . ." She stopped. It might sound brazen to tell him she wished she could be here all the time.

" 'E's happy with you," Jake said. "Used to bawl a terrible lot with her."

"His mother?"

Jake nodded. "She didn't bother with him. Hated this place right from the start. Couldn't wait to get back to Sydney."

111

"But it's lovely here," Tavy said, looking round. "It's so peaceful and . . ."

And how could anyone leave Joe, she thought, though she did not say it aloud.

'D'you think she'll ever come back?" she asked him.

He shook his head. "She'll never come back, not after what she did."

"You mean going with another man?"

"He's welcome to her. Not to my savings, though."

"You mean, they took all your money? Nothing left?"

"Only what's in here." He tapped the leather wallet slotted onto his belt. "That's all she left me."

"And Joe," Tavy added. "She left you with Joe."

Jake stood up, hitching his trousers. "You're right there, girl. It's Joe what matters." He looked down at them for a moment, sitting together on the grass. Then he turned and walked away to his vegetable patch.

Before Tavy left, she promised that she would come on Tuesday so that Jake could go to Burrawong Creek. Tomorrow was Sunday, Lily's half day, and on Monday there would be the ironing to do. It would take Jake all day to ride there and back and Tavy could not get away till the afternoon, but Joe could not yet climb out of his new cot and Wolf would keep guard outside the door. Jake was adamant about accepting her wages. He would just spend what he had, buy enough to keep them going until his vegetables were ready to sell. Then he would get his licence, take out a loan. After that, he would really set himself up, improve the house, buy a cow and some hens. It would not be long before he had sheep of his own.

Sunday was hot. Flies buzzed incessantly through morning prayers as the Master's voice droned on and on. Coming out into the courtyard afterwards, Tavy screwed up her eyes in the sudden glare. It's like heavenly fire, she thought, recalling a phrase from the lesson, although she had scarcely listened to it at all. Her mind had been full of her

112

talk with Jake. Fancy Joe's mother going off with all Jake's savings! What a baggage! Yet she must have been pretty for Jake to have liked her in the first place. Was she buxom and curvy like Lily and Annie Button from the *Henrietta*? Did she have pretty hair? Tavy had peeped through her fingers at Lily's yellow curls, at Louisa's glossy ringlets. She did wish hers was not quite so mouse. She would have liked Jake to notice her hair because lately she had begun to think differently about him. It had given her a funny feeling when he had looked at her yesterday while they were sitting under the trees. He had never really looked at her like that before, as if he thought she was a special sort of person. She hoped he would look at her that way again. Anyhow, she was determined to give him her money and somehow she would find time to run down with it before he left for Burrawong Creek on Tuesday morning.

When she had finished washing up the Sunday dinner, she went back to the bedroom and took the coins out of her drawstring bag. She decided to put them in an envelope —the one her testimonial was in would do nicely — because it would be easier to hand it to Jake all at once. She folded it over, neat and small, and put it away at the back of her drawer. Then she picked up her hairbrush and started to drag it through her hair. After a moment, she stopped and studied her reflection in the mirror. Her hair looked smoother, but it still did not shine. She tried again, bending over and brushing downwards, counting the strokes as Lily did. When she reached fifty, she stood up and inspected the result. Her face looked red and hot, her hair stuck out in a dull, mousy mop. She would just have to persevere. After all, Lily spent hours brushing hers every day, especially before she went to meet Harry. "It's my crowning glory," she told Tavy. "Well, that's what a certain person calls it." She had no doubt that Tavy knew who the certain person was, although they never discussed her affair with Harry openly. In the same way, Lily never questioned Tavy about her 'flying', though Tavy suspected Lily was not convinced that all Tavy wanted was space and freedom. "I reckon you've got some gentleman friend hidden in the bush," she teased Tavy. "Is it one of them big parrots or a great black Abo?" It was all just a joke and Tavy would chase her with a broom or whatever was at hand, but all the same she had a feeling that Lily was increasingly curious.

She decided to take the money down to Jake after tea on Monday and, when she ran back to fetch the envelope from her drawer, she unpinned her hair and brushed it, bending over and counting the strokes. Perhaps Jake would notice if it was soft and smooth.

"Whatever are you doing?" Lily stood in the door, looking at her in amazement.

"What d'you think I'm doing?" Tavy retorted, crimson-faced.

"Why've you got interested in your hair all of a sudden, Tavy? You don't usually care a brass farthing what you look like."

Tavy tossed her hair back. "Mind your own business, Lily. My hair's nothing to do with you."

"Hoity-toity, are we? You're not trying to pretty yourself up for some man, are you? It's not old Garrity, is it? Or Sam? I saw him having a look up your skirts the other day. Is it Sam you're sweet on?"

Tavy turned on her furiously. "Don't you dare say that! Never, never say that to me again!" She pounced on Lily, grabbing her 'crowning glory'. Lily twisted away and ran shrieking from the room, with Tavy in pursuit, till half way across the courtyard they heard "Stop that, you two harpies!" It was the stern voice of Mrs. O'Rourke.

"Jake."

He was coming round the corner of the hut with the milk pail. He looked up at Tavy and smiled as she ran along the path towards him, her hair flying round her face.

"I just wanted to give you this." She thrust the folded envelope towards him.

"What is it?"

"You'll see. Nothing much at all. How's Joe?"

"Joe's all right," he said, shaking the envelope. There was a chink of coins. She watched his face as he put down the milk pail and opened the packet.

"See here," he said, shaking out the money. "I told you, I'm not taking your earnings."

"Yes, you must. You won't have enough otherwise for all the things you need. There's the provisions and the rope for Wolf and clothes and . . ."

"Clothes?"

"Yes, clothes for Joe. His shirts don't fit and they're all worn out. You will try and get him some, won't you?"

She waited for him to answer, but he stood silent and frowning at the money.

"I can't stay now," she said. "I'll come tomorrow, as soon as I can."

As she turned to go, he caught her arm. " 'S not right this way; you keep it. You might need it."

"I don't need it, Jake, honest I don't. I get everything I want at Tallangatta. My boots don't wear out with no pavements to walk on, and I've enough clothes now because the Mistress gave me three dresses, so you see . . ." She stopped, noticing the way Jake was watching her.

"That's real pretty on you." He looked down at the green and white dimity. "Colour suits you a treat."

Tavy felt herself blush. "Please keep it, Jake," she said in a business-like voice, trying to pull her arm away. Jake tightened his grasp.

"No." He spoke firmly and slowly, his eyes on her face.

"But I must go now."

"Not till you take this back." He thrust the coins at her.

Tavy lifted her chin. She could be stubborn too.

"You can't give me orders. It's my money and I'm free to do what I want with it. If I want to give it to a friend, then . . ."

"A friend?"

"Yes," she retorted indignantly. Then she paused. "That's what I said," she added, with a touch of uncertainty.

He was frowning at her again.

Slowly a broad smile spread across his face. "Reckon that's what I really need," he said. "More'n all the shopping put together."

He let go of her arm and, lifting his hand, he touched her cheek with the tips of his fingers. Tavy looked back at him, her cheeks burning. Then she turned and ran quickly away.

Chapter Ten

Joe was wailing when Tavy arrived at the hut the next day. It was a mournful, hopeless kind of sound as if he despaired of anyone hearing, but he struggled to sit up when she opened the door, beaming through his tears when he saw her.

"Been on your own a long time, poor lovey," she said, picking him up.

Jake must have set off early for the hut was in more of a muddle than usual. The envelope she had put the money in was lying empty on the table. So he took it after all, she thought.

Joe was happy for the rest of the day, shunting himself round the hut while she worked, pestering Wolf who lay outside the door in the glaring sun, flies swarming over him and his heap of bones. Jake had shortened his rope, heeding Harry's warning, and he had little freedom to move away from Joe, who pulled his tail and poked him as if he were a toy. He bore Joe's assaults with surprising patience. He seemed to understand he must be gentle with him.

116

When the work was done, Tavy lay on the grass in the shade with Joe close to her, staring up through the trees at the deep, clear sky. I feel happiest here, she thought, because I'm free. And because I'm with Joe — and Jake? Yes, now she felt happy with Jake as well.

She stayed as late as she dared, only leaving when Joe fell asleep in his cot. As she hurried along the path to the creek, she saw a figure standing in the trees. It was a man, motionless. leaning on a stick with one leg bent at the knee resting on the other like a stork. He was dark skinned, with fuzzy hair and a beard, and she realised with a shock that he had nothing on at all except a necklace. For a moment they stared at each other and, although the man was several yards away, she could sense his calm stillness. There was a dignity about him as if he belonged there, where he stood, in the untamed bush. He must be an Abo, Tavy thought. Was he dangerous? Would Joe be all right? Should she go back? But Jake would be home soon and Wolf was there. He would be safe with Wolf and she ran quickly on.

"They're around all right," Jake said when she told him about the Abo she had seen the day before.

"Are they dangerous?"

"They don't like us white men. Can't blame 'em. It's their land."

She watched him hammering in a stake; he was adding a second row, about a foot from the first, laying timber between them to form a fence. Dust rose from the earth and hung in the air.

"Is that why you're building a fence, to keep the Abos out?"

"Sheep, more like." He grinned at her. "Don't want them trampling on my vegetables again. We've got to eat something besides stewed possum and 'roo."

It seemed the store keeper at Burrawong Creek had not been encouraging about selling Jake's produce.

"He reckoned folk grows what they want themselves.

Still, thanks to you, girl, I got enough stores to keep us going for a while." He went on hammering, avoiding her eye.

"Did you get everything?" Tavy asked. "Joe's shirts? Wolf's rope?"

"Yep, good strong bit, should hold him all right."

"And Joe's shirts?"

Jake didn't answer for a moment. Then he straightened and mopped his face.

"Money ran out. Anyways, he don't need shirts this weather. He can go bare; cooler that way."

"But he'll get sunburned," Tavy said. "Besides," she added primly, sounding like Cook at Cadogan Square, "he's not a little savage, you know."

She noticed Jake grin as she turned to go inside. The provisions had been dumped in a heap on the table. Joe knelt up in his cot, watching her sort them out and put them away in their respective tins.

"There's flour, Joe," she said. "That's for damper, and salt, and this must be sugar; this is nails, that's tea. But what are these bottles?"

She picked up a small straight-sided bottle of dark blue glass. On the label was written 'APLY to WOOND' in spidery print. The other was larger, with a cork in the top, and there was no label.

"It's lotion for stings," Jake told her, when she questioned him.

"And the other?" She waited, but he did not reply.

She went back into the hut and looked at it again. "I've seen enough bottles to know what this is," she said to Joe, standing it beside the lotion on the shelf above the fire. "Your Dada's spent that money on liquor for himself, and there you are dressed in nothing but rags. He's a selfish brute, Joe, that's what he is."

All the same, she knew better than to say so, however justified. 'Blathering on' might make him lose his temper again.

118

"It's you!"

Lily stood at the workroom door, holding a tray, staring at Tavy in surprise. Tavy closed the lid of the wicker basket and stood up. She looked back at Lily without a word.

"I saw the door open when I went to clear the tea and I know the Mistress likes it kept shut. Did she send you for something?"

Tavy shook her head.

"What are you doing then?" Lily's gaze moved to something white lying on the floor by the basket. She put the tray on the sewing table and went to pick it up. It was a small lace-trimmed jacket embroidered with flowers. "It's a baby's," she said, frowning at it. Then she looked at Tavy. "What do you want baby clothes for?" Her eyes moved slowly from Tavy's face down to her apron. "You're not . . .? Tavy, you don't mean to tell me you're . . . ?"

Tavy snatched the little jacket away with a contemptuous snort. "How dare you even think such a thing! You may be one of them girls what behaves like that, but I'm not. I'm decent and respectable and honest . . ."

She stopped suddenly, glancing down at the jacket in her hand. Honest? Was it honest to think of taking — well, borrowing some of the baby clothes without asking the Mistress? Of course, she would have put them back when Joe had finished with them, so it was not really stealing but it was half way there.

"What d'you want them for, then?" Lily persisted.

"I'm not taking them, Lily," she said, making up her mind. They were too flimsy for Joe, anyway. He would just have to go on wearing his shabby little shirts. "I was only looking at them." There she was telling lies now. "Don't you dare tell the Mistress about it. You won't, will you?" she added anxiously. "Please don't, Lily."

"Not if you tell me why you were nosing into that basket. There must be a reason. I mean, all of a sudden you're brushing your hair much more, then looking for baby clothes. It's no wonder I'm getting ideas, is it?"

"My hair's got nothing whatever to do with it," Tavy

stated. "And the clothes were just for a baby who's not got much to wear but I'm not taking them anyway. I've told you that already." She folded the little jacket and put it back into the basket.

"But you were thinking of it," Lily said triumphantly. "Where is the baby then?"

"What's it to you?"

"I want to know, that's all. Come on, Tavy, or I'll tell the Mistress on you."

Tavy opened her mouth.

"Well?" Lily prompted.

"You know the bushman by the creek?"

"Yes." Lily took a step closer. listening eagerly.

"Well, it's his."

"His baby!" Lily opened his eyes wide. "You mean, that woman left the baby behind when she ran off with the traveller?"

Tavy nodded. "He's still there and he's ever so sweet and his shirts are all raggedy and too small and . . ."

"Well!" Lily exclaimed. "Makes you wonder, don't it? I mean, fancy there being a baby down there all this time and nobody even knowing about it excepting for you, Tavy. So that's where you go when you're flying, is it?"

"Yes. But just to look after the baby." There was no need for Lily to get ideas about her and Jake.

"What about the bushman?" Lily asked, as if she could read Tavy's thoughts.

"Oh, he doesn't pay no heed to me," Tavy told her, closing the lid of the basket firmly. "And if you split on me, Lily, I can get my own back. What about you and Master Harry? You needn't think I haven't noticed that."

The heat was unrelenting now. Only on the voyage out had Tavy known sun so powerful. Each morning the early sky, lucid and pale, intensified to a deep clear blue. Dust blew in drifts across the plain, powdering the tussocks of dry grass. The Mistress's lawn lost its fresh green and her English

120

flowers drooped and died. Lily and Tavy got up at dawn to iron and polish while it was still cool. Mrs. O'Rourke did her baking then; mince pies, fruit cakes, spice cookies and candied plums sat in neat rows on the store room shelf.

"But who will eat all that?" Tavy asked. The heat took her appetite away.

"Oh, everyone likes a good tuck in at Christmas," Mrs. O'Rourke told her.

Christmas? How could it be Christmas in weather like this?

In the afternoons, Tallangatta lay silent and still in the scorching glare. The family rested, Bron, the old sheep dog, flopped in the shade, Mrs. O'Rourke slept in her rocking chair, her bottle of 'physic' close at hand. It was easy for Tavy to slip down to the hut, particularly now that Lily knew where she went, although she was never quite sure how much she could trust her not to mention it to Harry. "Flying to your baby?" she would inquire as she lay on her bed and brushed her hair.

Tavy would put a finger to her lips. "You promised to keep it a secret, Lily."

"All right, I know," Lily would answer with a grin.

She seldom saw Sam these days, for the rams had been moved over near the woolshed. After the shearing, the shepherds had taken the rest of the stock back to open pasture and the orchard paddocks were empty.

Jake worked through the heat, felling timber to complete his fence. Each tree that came down left the bush beyond the clearing more open, easier to see through, and once or twice Tavy thought she saw figures standing a little way off. Were they Abos or shadows? They stood so still. Perhaps she was just imagining it. Then Jake told her he had seen the Abos' fire in the dark. "Reckon they've got a camp not far from here," he said. "They make for the creeks in weather like this. Means their water holes in the bush are dry."

But the level of the creek had fallen too. Jake carted buckets of water for his vegetables, pouring it carefully, not wasting a drop. Tavy admired them. "They look ever so good."

"Not too bad," Jake said proudly patting a pumpkin.

Tavy went barefoot when she was at the hut, hitching up her skirts to let the sun brown her legs. She didn't feel shy with Jake any more. But how shocked Mr. Lutterworth would be, she thought, and she laughed aloud. Cadogan Square seemed a lifetime ago. Sometimes she carried Joe to the creek, where he sat naked in the water, splashing and squealing, while she dabbled her toes and fanned the mosquitoes away from his head. Each day, the creek grew shallower. What would Jake do if it dried completely? But surely this weather must break soon. In the evenings, she went and stared across the flat, empty plain, searching for signs of rain. Occasionally, long feathers of cloud drifted over the horizon, turning pink in the lowering sun, but before long they had disappeared.

"D'you think it will rain?" she asked Garrity whenever she saw him, and he always answered, "Not yet, not yet."

The orchard was the coolest place, shaded all day by the thick foliage of the trees. Tavy liked to go there after supper and walk barefoot through the long grass to pick an orange and suck out the juice. Bron often followed her, lumbering slowly, stiff with age. One evening, as she stopped at the gate to put on her boots, she noticed Bron prick up his ears and sniff the air.

"What is it, boy?" she said. Then she saw Sam coming up through the empty paddocks. He paused when he noticed her, and for a moment they both stared at each other before Tavy twisted away and ran back towards the homestead, with her unbuttoned boots flapping round her ankles.

"Oh, Jake!"

Tavy gazed in horror at the vegetable patch. The carefully tended cabbages, the pumpkins, turnips and potatoes were battered and crushed.

"Poor Jake," she said. "And you worked so hard."

Jake shrugged, without turning round, but she could tell he was distressed. She watched him raking the roughened soil.

"Was it sheep again?"

"This weren't animals. They'd have eaten the greens, churned up the earth with their hoofs. Didn't hear nothing. Must have been last night when I were inside."

"Could it have been the Abos?"

He straightened, leaning on his rake, prodding a broken cabbage with his toe. "Dunno. Ground's too dry to see footprints, but this ain't the sort of stuff they go for. They'll pinch animals for meat, but not vegetables 'cos mostly they eat what they find in the bush: lilly-pilly berries, them witchety grubs and such like. Reckon me and Joe'll be living on the same pretty soon," he added bitterly.

"Is it all ruined then?"

"Oh, some of the roots should be all right, tatties and turnips. Suppose we'll manage."

"I'll bring you some fruit, Jake," Tavy said eagerly. "There's so much in the Campions' orchard. Lots of it just lies in the grass going rotten, so nobody minds if I take some of that."

"Be good if you can. Joe likes fruit, gobbled up them cherries you brought, and the apricots too."

"Yes, he loved them didn't he? The oranges are ripe now and they're nice and juicy."

"What's up?" Jake asked, noticing her frown.

She shook her head. "It's nothing — at least . . .," she hesitated. "No, nothing, really."

It would not help to tell him that talking of oranges had reminded her of the evening before when she had seen Sam coming up through the paddocks. It had been growing dark. Jake would have been inside by then. She remembered the conversation she had overheard between Master Harry and his father. "I'll tell Sam to keep an eye on him,' Master Harry had said, and the Master's reply 'without aggravating the situation'. But Sam, with his grudge against Jake, would not be averse to trampling all over Jake's vegetables while he carried out Master Harry's instructions, nor would he bother to mention what he had done when he reported that now the bushman was building a fence right round his clearing.

"It just doesn't feel like Christmas to me," Tavy said, tying a red ribbon round a spray of evergreen. "It's so hot."

She and Lily were decorating the drawing room. Branches of prickly grevillea and banksia lay strewn about the floor.

"Always is hot at Christmas," Lily said. "What d'you expect?"

"Cold," Tavy said. "Snow sometimes, not this. It doesn't seem right."

For the first time since she had left England, she was longing for home. Christmas at Saint Agatha's had been far from lavish, but the anticipation, the growing excitement had coloured the frugal festivities; the one present handed out by the Chairman of the Governors, the bag of sweets, the carol singing. And the dinner. How they had enjoyed the roast pork, the plum pudding and custard, as well as mince pies. In the evening, they had all listened to Aunt Lavender reading the story of Christmas. It was the part about the star that Tavy liked best. The star of Bethlehem. There was magic in the words and she whispered them to herself as she stared out of the window, looking for the first star shining in the frosty darkness. The magic had come back every Christmas. Even last year, when she had been almost grown up and about to leave and go out in the world, it had not lost its hold on her. She sighed now, remembering.

"Oh, I know how you feel, Tavy," Lily said, standing on the couch to stick a bough of grevillea behind a portrait of Grandfather Campion. "Last year was my first Christmas away from home, but we had ever such a good time. Oops!" The springs of the couch sagged under Lily's weight. She flung down the grevillea and jumped off, just as the door opened and the Mistress came in.

"Oh, doesn't it look a picture!" She gazed round, smiling delightedly.

"But Mama, it isn't nearly enough," Louisa said, coming in behind her. She snatched the spray of banksia from Lily's hands and forced it down behind the top of the cabinet.

"Careful, dearest," her mother warned.

"I am careful, Mama." She selected two or three more branches and ran round the room poking them in wherever there was a space. "There, that is a little better. We must have plenty. Garrity must cut more, much more. Here." She thrust a bough at Tavy, who was standing on the piano stool. "Put this above the mirror. No, not there, higher, higher, right at the top," she urged, as Tavy stretched up on tiptoe trying to reach. Proper Miss Bossyboots, aren't you, Tavy thought, jumping down and watching Louisa who was flying round again rearranging Lily and Tavy's decorations. She was excited, roused from her boredom by the prospect of festivities. She would play her Mozart sonata in front of all the staff when they came to be presented with their gifts. After that, she would sing 'I saw three ships a-sailing by', at least five verses, and then she would curtsy and everyone would clap. She had a new gown to wear, pale yellow muslin with ribbons to match, which would make those silly servant girls exceedingly jealous.

"She's so full of herself, she might pop," Lily remarked when she and Tavy were back in the kitchen. But it was Mrs. O'Rourke who looked as if she would pop. Crimson-faced and gleaming, she chopped and stirred, beat, iced, larded, stuffed, tasted and tasted again, with frequent nips of 'physic' to keep her indigestion at bay. "Out of my way," she ordered, waving a spoon at Tavy and "Don't you dare be touching that!" she bellowed at Lily, who had a weakness for picking off crumbs and dipping her finger into bowls when she thought Mrs. O'Rourke wasn't looking.

"Makes me so hungry, though," Lily said. "Oh, I do love Christmas feasting. Only two more days! I can't wait."

"Nobody's asking you to stand around waiting, my girl,

Mrs. O'Rourke told her. "There's more than enough to do."

It was true. For the next two days, Lily and Tavy scuttled round the homestead cleaning and polishing, running back and forth across the courtyard to the kitchen, the dairy, the cold store, the laundry, this way and that until at last, the supper dishes done, they flopped exhausted on their beds. There was no possible chance of going to the hut. Is Joe all right, Tavy thought as she worked. Was Jake managing without her help? He wouldn't leave Joe alone for long, with the Abos so close. Was there still enough water in the creek? Even the deep water holes here at Tallangatta were getting low now. "Don't you be wasting it," warned Mrs. O'Rourke.

"Do we have time off on Christmas Day?" Tavy asked Lily.

"Gracious, no. It's busy as anything. There's churchify-ings in the morning. That takes a long time. Then, there's family dinner and when we've finished washing up, it's the staff party."

"The party?" Tavy said.

"Yes. We all go, Garrity, Sam, the shepherds, the Master gives out presents and we have punch and sweetmeats and mince pies, and we all sing carols and . . ."

"But after that," Tavy said. "Aren't we free after that?"

Lily opened her eyes wide. "Oh, but after that it's the best part of all. We have our dinner then. It's a real feast and you can eat as much as you like. I thought I'd burst last year. There's always lots left over for Boxing Day too."

"Boxing Day," Tavy echoed hopefully. "In England, Boxing Day is a holiday."

"Oh, it is here, too," Lily said. "Well, once we've finished clearing up, it is."

Chapter Eleven

"Jake, Jake."

Tavy ran across the clearing, carrying her carpet bag. He turned round, watching her come towards him.

"Hello, girl," he said. "Joe and me was wondering when you'd come."

"I'm sorry, truly I am. I wanted to come, but there was so much to do with Christmas and everything and . . ."

"Christmas?" Jake looked puzzled. "When is it?"

Tavy laughed. "Yesterday. It's over. Didn't you know?" But then, why should he have known?

"Oh, reckoned it might come up sometime soon. There was talk of it over at Burrawong Creek. Don't pay much heed to what date it is here." He paused a moment before he added, "Shame though, missing Christmas. Never done that before."

"But you haven't missed it all," Tavy said. "I mean, today's Boxing Day and that's special too."

"Well, there ain't much I can do about it any rate," Jake said. "Damper and dripping with a turnip thrown in for a treat. Meat's gone off. That possum I caught's as high as old socks, and there's precious little game around with the Abos after everything. But it don't bother Joe. So long as the goat keeps giving milk, he'll be all right. Full of beans, he is, into every damn thing."

"I'll go and see to him," Tavy said, noticing that Jake was eyeing her bag, and hurrying away before he could ask her what she had brought.

"Yes, you are into everything, you rascal," she said, removing Joe from her carpet bag for the third time. "Here — you play with this." She gave him a tin plate and a spoon. "There's a secret in my bag and I'm not going to show you or your Dada what it is till the work's done."

"Agoo," Joe said. He had learned a new sound each time she came.

She talked to him while she was cleaning, mixing the damper, milking the goat and washing the clothes, telling him that they mustn't waste a drop of water because the creek was almost dry. When she had finished and everything was ready, she picked Joe up and went to the door.

"Jake!" she called.

"What's up?" he shouted, without looking round.

"Surprise. Come and see."

He put down his axe and she watched him come slowly across the parched grass, trying to hide her excitement.

"Well, what's up?" he said again, mopping the sweat from his face.

She stepped aside so that he could see through the open door behind her.

"Happy Christmas," she said.

"Agoo," said Joe. But for several moments Jake said nothing at all. He ducked under the lintel, taking off his hat and stood gazing at the table. Then he looked at Tavy. His eyes were shining.

"It's a Christmas party," he said. "Don't that look good?"

Tavy sighed happily. She had to admit that it did look festive, with two small parcels wrapped in red paper, and the food she had brought set out on plates. There was cold goose and sausage, a hunk of plum pudding, three mince pies (which had got rather battered in the carpet bag), a lump of curd cheese and a slice of fruit cake. In the middle was a mug of white and yellow flowers she had found near the creek, surrounded by oranges and dark shiny leaves.

Jake beamed at her, then he turned to Joe. "Your first Christmas, Joe. How about that?"

Joe bounced up and down in Tavy's arms.

128

"Can't wait to get at it, can you, son?" Jake said, tossing his hat into the corner. "But I got to get myself smart for a party."

He kicked off his boots, washed his face behind the hut, put on his shirt, even ran his fingers through his dusty, matted hair.

"Now," he said, sitting down and helping himself to his first plateful.

Tavy held Joe on her lap, handing him small pieces of food which he crammed in his mouth, appearing to enjoy it as much as Jake.

Every so often, Jake glanced up at him. "Real good tucker, eh Joe?" he said with his mouth full, and each time his plate was empty, Tavy refilled it.

"You have some too, girl," he urged, noticing that she wasn't eating.

"I had my share yesterday. Honest, Jake, there was so much food, heaps of it left over even after we'd had dinner and the men took away as much as they wanted. We put a whole lot back on the store room shelf but Mrs. O'Rourke, she's the Campions' cook, said it wouldn't all keep and she told me to throw the rest in the bin."

"Must be plum crazy, ditching tucker like this," Jake mumbled through a mouthful of mince pie.

"I didn't throw it out, though," she said, popping another raisin in Joe's mouth. "I hid it till they all went down to the woolshed. They was there half the night, boozing and singing and dancing, so no one saw me put it in my bag. And it weren't stealing really, saving it from going to waste," she added to justify her action in Jake's eyes.

He chuckled. "Downright common sense, if you ask me," he said.

While he went on eating, she told him about what Lily called 'churchifyings' in the morning that went on for what seemed like hours, with Mrs. O'Rourke nodding off and snoring, 'quite loud it were too' and Lily, the other maid servant, making eyes at Master Harry 'because she's sweet on him, you see'. She paused as Jake glanced at her across the table, and she felt him move his foot against her bare leg. To hide her confusion, she put Joe on the floor and cleared away some of the empty dishes. Then, picking up the larger of the two parcels, she placed it in front of Jake.

"What's this?" he said.

"Your present." She spoke briskly, lest he should think she was behaving like Lily. "You've been too busy eating to notice it."

"Thought those was part of the decorations," he said, grinning at her and wiping his mouth on his sleeve.

"Go on," she said, "Open it. And this one's for you, lovey." She knelt on the floor, handing Joe the other parcel.

Jake looked down at Tavy, with Joe beside her sucking the red ribbon.

"Why are you so good to us, girl?" he asked.

She glanced up at him, turning away quickly because she suddenly felt shy. "It's Christmas, that's all," she said. "Presents is part of Christmas." She helped Joe tear the red paper off his parcel while, slowly and carefully, Jake unwrapped his. Inside Joe's was a string of green glass beads.

"Pretty," Tavy said, lifting them so that they caught the light and Joe clutched at them, crowing with delight.

" 'E's pleased with them all right," Jake said. "And me too. Candy fruit, all sweet and sugary. If that ain't just what I like."

Both the beads and the candied fruit had been given to her yesterday when, in the afternoon, everyone — Garrity, Sam and the shepherds as well — had squeezed into the drawing room for the party. One by one, as the Master called their names, they had gone up to receive their parcels. As well as a box of candied fruit, Lily had also been given beads, though hers were blue. She had put them on at once, lifting her hair to show off her white neck while Tavy fastened the clasp. Then she had fondled them, clinking them together, watching Harry out of the corner of her eye to make sure he was noticing. "You wear yours too," she had said to Tavy and, as she put them round her neck, Tavy had seen Louisa nudge Harry and whisper in his ear. There was rum punch and mince pies and subdued conversation till Louisa, seating herself at the piano and arranging her yellow muslin skirts round her, had played her Mozart sonata. When she curtsied, there had been a scatter of clapping, led by the Mistress, then shuffling and coughing and clearing of throats until Louisa had started again with a rendering of 'I saw three ships'. The thin high sound seemed to vibrate through the suffocating room, and the stench of sweat mingling with the aromatic smell of evergreen had made Tavy desperate to escape into the space and cool air. "On Christmas Day, on Christmas Day," sang Louisa's quavering voice. But it's not, Tavy had thought, it's not Christmas at all.

Yet the strange thing was that now, only one day later, though it was still just as hot and they were only eating leftovers in a primitive hut, she did have a Christmassy kind of feeling. She looked at Joe playing with his beads, then she looked at Jake and smiled.

"Happy Christmas," he said and he picked out a candied cherry and offered it to her.

"They're for you," she said, but she opened her mouth and let him pop it in.

He got up and went outside to untie Wolf's rope. "Not much left for you, poor old dog," he said, throwing Wolf the scraps. Wolf pounced on them eagerly, sniffing round for more.

Then Jake fetched the larger of the two bottles from the shelf above the hearth. He uncorked it and poured a little into a mug.

"Try that," he said, passing it to Tavy.

She sniffed it and wrinkled her nose at him. "Rum?"

"Yep. Go on, taste it."

She hesitated. She had been angry when he had bought it rather than clothes for Joe and here was the poor little love still in rags. But, well, it was Christmas and all men like a drink now and then. She remembered Tom Grundy had liked his quart of ale, Duggan had been partial to a tankard of grog. And Jake had hardly made a habit of it — not when you compared him with Sam or Willie Moser. She took a cautious sip.

"Ah." She stuck her tongue out, passing back the mug. "Takes me breath away."

Jake laughed. "Don't you like it?"

"It's like fire-water. You have it."

He took a mouthful and sat back, savouring the taste. "That's good," he said.

Joe looked up. "Agoo," he said.

Jake and Tavy laughed.

"It is good, son. You feel like a drop?"

Tavy stood up quickly. "No, Jake. He's much too small."

Jake shook his head. "Don't worry, girl. I were only teasing. Come on, let's go outside." He lifted Joe onto his shoulders and, picking up the bottle and the candied fruits, he went across the clearing.

Tavy looked at the dirty dishes. Should she clear them straight away? But no, it was Christmas. They could wait till later on.

Jake was lying in the shade, propped on one elbow, while Joe clambered over him babbling in his own private language.

"Like Christmas, do you, Joe?" Jake was saying as Tavy sat beside them. "Well, reckon this is the best one I've had myself since I come to Australia." He glanced up at Tavy and she guessed that the remark was meant for her.

"Was that a long time ago?"

"Five years or so."

"Where from?"

"Yorkshire."

"My friend Annie Button came from Yorkshire too. Why d'you pick on Australia?"

Jake took a mouthful of rum. It seemed to loosen his tongue.

"Just happened that way. My Pa worked down the mines. There was nine of us in a cottage not much bigger than that hut. We used to walk three miles to school, there and back. Hard going it were on the edge of the moors, with the rain

132

and the wind like the blade of a knife. But summer, that were different. Oftentimes in summer we didn't go to school at all."

"What did you do instead?" Tavy asked.

"Went poaching and fishing, stole birds' eggs. We was always up to something, me and me brothers. The girls was all right, but us three boys ..." He paused, smiling to himself, remembering it. "Mum was too worn out just feeding us all to pay much heed but Pa used to give us such a hiding we couldn't sit down for days on end. Real strict he was. Sent us boys down the pits when we turned twelve."

"That must have been awful," Tavy said. "Under the ground and all in the dark."

Jake took another swig at his rum. "Just like hell is, I reckon."

"And the lower deck of a ship too," Tavy said, lifting Joe onto her lap, and she told Jake about the *Henrietta*, how ill she had been and how she had found a secret place on deck where she could hide, because she hated it so much down below.

"Yep," Jake agreed. "It's bad under there when the seas turn rough, but I worked my passage and it's bad up the rigging too, hanging on for your life."

"But there was air to breathe," Tavy pointed out. "And space and sky."

Jake looked at her with surprise. "D'you feel that way too?"

She nodded. "Mm. Room to stretch out. That matters to me. I suppose that's why I came to Australia. I'd never been any place but London before, never seen sky when it weren't full of smoke." She lifted her head and stared at the vivid blue between the trees. "Not like this. This goes on and on till, well, till it feels like you're up there too. And at night the stars, they're so huge and bright, different from in England, kind of upside down."

Jake laughed. "They're not the same stars as up north. I learned a bit about them when I was in the ship. Sailors can steer by the stars, you know."

"Yes." Duggan had told her that. He had been rather like Jake, come to think of it, solid and steady and he never said much either. This was the first time Jake had really talked to her, the first chance she had had to find out about him. Perhaps it was Christmas, or perhaps it was the rum, but whatever it was she wanted him to go on talking. "Were you a miner for a long time?" she said, prompting him to go on.

"Till I were eighteen. Then my Pa got sick with dust in his lungs, used to cough his guts up, poor devil. Too much for my Ma, it were, so I gave her my savings and went south to Bristol. Worked in the docks for a couple of years. They were a rough lot them dockers, boozing and fighting, and their women were the same."

Tavy cradled Joe in her arms, waving off the flies. He was growing sleepy.

"Why d'you come here?" she asked.

"One of me mates heard tell of a ship that needed a crew. Seemed like a good chance to get away and Australia sounded fine: land, jobs, money. Only it weren't like that when I got to Sydney."

"I know," Tavy said. "I hated it too. Did you stay for long?"

"Oh, I worked in the docks again for a while, just to make a bit of money and, well, I got mixed up with a girl." He paused, running his fingers along Joe's bare leg. "I'd been six months at sea. That's a fair old time for a man, you know."

Tavy said nothing. Was the girl Joe's mother, she wanted to ask. What was she like, plump and pretty with red gold hair? She glanced up at Jake, hoping he would go on.

"She was all right till she got in the family way," he said, tugging at a tough stalk of grass. "Then she started blathering on, wanting this and that, better tucker, bigger house, pretty clothes, nothing were right. Spent all my savings on the horse and we went south. I found work on a property near Parramatta, good place it were." He chewed the grass stalk, remembering.

Tavy looked at him. It was wrong to get a girl in the family

134

way. Aunt Lavender would be shocked, most people would. But Jake was not a bad sort of man. He was gentle and honest, someone you could trust.

"I liked it there," he said, "working with sheep. Learned a lot too. Joe was born, and things were fine for a while. The Mistress up at the homestead were real good to us and the girl were busy enough with Joe. Then she got sick of it, started complaining again, wanting a place of our own."

He drained his mug and lay back, his arms folded behind his head. Joe was sucking his thumb, almost asleep.

"So then what?" Tavy asked.

"Came on here. Lucky to find it, I reckoned; good run alongside the creek, and I worked real hard clearing the bush, splitting logs for the hut. Built it good and solid, pretty fast too, but she weren't happy here." He sighed. "Right from the start, she were full of complaints, always at me, and Joe crying and crying till she near murdered the little beggar. Made me mad to see how she treated him. We was always fighting. It were good riddance when she went."

He closed his eyes. Tavy knew the rest. How she had ridden away on the traveller's horse, taking Jake's savings and leaving Joe.

"Weren't the life for her," Jake said in a drowsy voice. "And I weren't the man for her neither." He opened his eyes and looked up at Tavy. "She weren't like you, girl. Not one scrap – but for one thing." He stretched out his hand and touched Tavy's hair. "She had pretty hair, kind of brown and smooth, goldy in the sun, just like yours."

Pretty hair, me, pretty hair! She shook it over her face, turning her head away from Jake's gentle smile because her happiness was almost too much to bear. When she glanced back, he was still watching her.

"Used to reckon Joe and me would be fine on our own but now, well, not sure I were right."

For a while she just sat there, letting his words echo in her head, sensing the stillness, the peace of the place, without trying to work out the full meaning of what Jake had said. Later on she would think about it, keep on thinking about it, with a warm feeling deep inside her like a special present you keep, taking it out to look at it again and again. It was a Christmas present, yes, her present from Jake. He had closed his eyes again, breathing steadily. She got up quietly and carried Joe inside for a rest.

She had almost finished clearing up the Christmas feast when she heard the clop of horse's hoofs on the hard ground. Through the half open door, she saw Harry riding into the clearing and behind him, tied to a rope, was a skinny brown dog. It was Wolf. He had got away! Then she remembered Jake had untied him to give him the scraps. He had been loose in the hut and they had forgotten all about him. She watched Harry dismount. He hooked the reins over a stake, looked round the clearing then, jerking Wolf after him, he strode over to where Jake lay under the trees.

"Bushman." His voice cracked like a gun shot through the stillness.

Jake sat up, staring at Harry, befuddled with sleep.

Harry dragged Wolf forward so that Tavy heard a choking sound come from the dog's throat.

"This your cur?"

Jake rubbed his eyes, then heaved himself to his feet. Wolf cowered on the grass, whimpering.

"This yours?" Harry repeated, impatiently.

"Wha's 'e doing wi' you?" Jake's speech was slurred.

"Doing with me! What the hell was he doing on my land? I've warned you that, if I catch him chasing sheep, I'll shoot him. I'm a fair man, Bushman, and you can count yourself lucky that I found him before he got at the stock. But you won't get another chance, I can tell you for sure." He prodded Wolf with the toe of his boot and thrust the rope at Jake. "Tie him up, Bushman, and keep him under control."

Jake glared at Harry without moving.

"Tie him up, do you hear?"

With his eyes on Harry, Jake reached out for the rope, missing it, grasping at nothing. Then he snatched at it angrily.

136

"Who d'you think you are, Campion, barging in here . . ."

"Tie him up." Harry's tone was menacing.

Muttering under his breath, Jake blundered to a tree and tied the rope round it. Harry strolled over and inspected the knot. Then he untied it, doubled it round Wolf's neck so that it was half the length and knotted it firmly.

"Call yourself a bushman. You can't even tie a rope." Harry turned to Jake, who stood head thrust forward, fists clenched. For a moment they faced each other then, as Harry stepped back, his boot struck something hard. He bent and picked up the rum bottle lying at his feet.

Jake made a grab at it. "Give me that."

Harry laughed and swung the bottle away from him, holding it up to see how much it contained.

"No wonder you were sleeping soundly! Want the dregs? Here, catch." He tossed it suddenly at Jake, who fumbled, letting it slip to the ground.

"You devil!" Jake growled, but Harry wasn't listening. Tavy saw that he was staring at something in the grass. Jake's eyes followed his gaze, but Harry moved fast. "And not only the drink!" There was a note of triumph in his voice as he held up something green that sparkled in the sunlight.

Tavy gasped, her hands to her face. Joe's beads, her beads. Did Harry recognise them?

"I understood your lady friend deserted you some time ago, Bushman. I am surprised that you have not found these before." There was a pause while Harry frowned at the beads. Even from inside the hut, Tavy could feel the tension grow. She heard the chink as Harry coiled them into his palm. He looked up at Jake.

"Have you perhaps found yourself someone different now? I wonder where you manage to do so in a remote place like this." His tone was sarcastic. "Unless I am much mistaken, I have seen these beads before. They belong to one of our servant girls, a Christmas gift from my mother. I recall her wrapping them — blue beads for the pretty girl, green for . . ." he paused, "for the other. Am I not right?"

"Mind your own damn business," Tavy heard Jake growl.

"She happens to be in my father's employment," Harry retorted. "Her welfare is our business. Is she here now?"

He glanced at the hut. Tavy cowered behind the door, her mouth dry with fear. Jake was silent.

"I demand an answer. Is the girl here?"

Still Jake said nothing.

"I have no wish for a scene, Bushman. Fetch her out and I'll take her back with me." Harry turned and walked towards his horse. He was behind it now, unhitching the reins, with his back to the hut. "And in future keep your hands off our servants and keep that dog . . ."

But Tavy did not wait to hear any more. Snatching up her boots, she darted out of the door, round the corner of the hut and away with dread in her heart.

Chapter Twelve

"I have something here that belongs to you, Octavia."

Tavy glanced up. The Mistress was holding her beads.

"My son, Harry, found them outside the bushman's hut. Did you know they were there?"

"Yes, ma'am," Tavy said in a small voice.

The Mistress handed her the beads. "I hope you will be more careful with them now, Octavia. They were my Christmas present to you."

Tavy felt her face go crimson. "Thank you, ma'am," she whispered, accepting the beads without looking up.

"Octavia, do you remember that I told you on no account

were you to go near the run beyond the creek?"

Tavy nodded.

"Then why did you do so?"

There was a long silence while Tavy twisted the beads round her fingers, concentrating on their bright green circles above the dark red squares of the drawing room carpet. . .

A trickle of sweat ran down her cheek.

"Will you kindly answer my question."

Tavy took a deep breath. "Because of the baby, ma'am." The words came out in a rush.

"Baby? Did you say baby?"

"Yes, ma'am."

Tavy looked up. The Mistress was frowning, her head on one side. "Octavia, do I understand you to mean that the bushman still has the baby there, that the woman left her child behind?"

"That's right, ma'am. That's why I go, so as to help look after him."

"You have been frequently?"

"Well, well yes, I suppose you could say that. But I haven't neglected my duties, ma'am. I've always done me work here before I went."

"I have no complaints on that score, Octavia. I am, however, surprised that you have continually disobeyed my instructions in such a deceitful manner. Are you not ashamed of yourself?"

Tavy did not answer.

"Well, Octavia?"

Tavy lifted her chin and looked the Mistress straight in the eye. "No, ma'am, I'm not. Someone had to look after Joe. It would have been wicked of me if I hadn't, worse than being disobedient to you, ma'am, much worse. You'd think so too if you saw him, ma'am. He's ever so sweet and that was why I took these beads for him because he . . ."

The Mistress held up her hand. "Just a moment, Octavia. How did you discover that the baby was there in the first place?"

Tavy looked surprised. Then she realised the Campions had never known that she had been left at Jake's hut instead of Tallangatta. The Mistress listened attentively while Tavy told her what had happened, taking care not to mention that she had spent a night at the hut. "As soon as ever I found out I was in the wrong place, I came straight up here, ma'am, but I couldn't stop thinking about Joe. He's such a little love, really he is, and it bothered me knowing he was on his own so much. That was why I went back, you see."

The Mistress nodded thoughtfully. "Octavia, did you never think of talking to me about this baby?" Her voice was gentle now. "I am not an unreasonable person, you know."

"Oh, I do know, ma'am. You're ever so kind." Tavy saw that the Mistress was smiling. "But all the same, ma'am, you'd have forbid me to go there, wouldn't you?"

The Mistress did not answer. Instead, she stood up and walked to the door. "Come with me, Octavia," she said as she opened it and went out. Tavy followed her along the passage to the work room.

"Now," said the Mistress, going over to the cot, "there is this dear little bed, there is that baby bath, the rocking horse and many other toys, there is a perambulator and this basket full of clothes; everything a baby needs. Tomorrow, you will come with me in the spring cart and we will collect the baby and bring him here. I shall speak to the bushman myself and explain that it will be greatly to the baby's advantage. I am sure he will understand."

Tavy looked round the room. Yes, everything Joe needed was here. But would Jake understand? Would he see it that way? He loved Joe so much. On the other hand, now that Joe could crawl Jake could no longer leave him. The hut was not a safe place for a baby and there were Abos in the woods nearby. Jake was finding it difficult to give Joe the food he needed and the creek was almost dry. He would have good food here and, though the water holes were low, there was still enough. It would certainly be better for Joe to come here. And it would not be for ever, only for a few months until . . .

140

"Well, Octavia, take that frown off your face," the Mistress said, breaking into Tavy's thoughts. "The matter is quite settled, and most happily I should say. I shall delight in having a baby here again and I have no doubt that Louisa will find it most diverting."

Louisa! With Joe! Louisa finding him diverting, as if he were some kind of toy! Tavy shook her head. "It wouldn't do, ma'am. Truly, it wouldn't do at all. You see Jake loves him, loves him very much. He'd never let him go, ma'am, and not because he's selfish. He's not a bad man like you think, he's decent and gentle and . . ." Tears welled into her eyes, she gulped back a sob and suddenly she turned and ran from the room.

"I don't see why you're so bothered," Lily said to Tavy, who sat on her bed with her head in her hands. "Why not fetch him here if the Mistress says she'll have him."

"No, Lily, I can't." She had tried and tried to explain, but Lily could not understand that Jake would never part with Joe.

"Downright cruel, if you ask me," Lily said, "keeping a dear little baby in a place like that. But still, with you not helping look after it any more, perhaps he'll see sense, go away and find himself some other woman to look after it and him as well. That'd be good if he did, seeing as how Master Harry wants his land. Let's hope he'll do that, eh? Good gracious, now what's the matter?" she asked in exasperation, for Tavy had flung herself face down on the bed, sobbing aloud.

That evening had been like a nightmare. The news that she had been looking after the bushman's baby had spread round Tallangatta like fire. But however much she longed to, it was no good hiding herself away. There was her work to be done and she had to carry on as usual, helping Lily to serve the supper, noticing the conversation die as she went into the dining room, the pointed way in which everyone avoided looking at her. Everyone, that is, except Louisa. She kept glancing at Tavy's tear-blotched face, then sideways at Harry, who sat next to her, but for once, to Tavy's small relief, he took no notice of his sister, staring sternly ahead. He had guessed Tavy had been at the hut that afternoon. Had he seen her run away? Or had he continued to demand that Jake fetch her out then, discovering she had gone, feel he had been made to look a fool? At least he could not have searched for her inside, because he had not known about Joe.

Mrs. O'Rourke had been so flabbergasted by the news that she had been forced to take an extra nip of her 'physic' before supper. "Upsets me digestion, a sudden shock like that," she had said. "Whoever would have believed there was a baby down there all this time, and Tavy after hopping off to look after it without a word to anyone at all."

There had been an explosive snort from Lily that had turned into a sneeze. "It's the dust," she had explained, winking at Tavy. But Tavy was not in a winking kind of mood.

The next morning, the Mistress called Tavy to the drawing room. When she knocked and went in, she saw Louisa was there.

"Take Bron round the garden for a little walk before it gets too warm, dearest."

"But, Mama, you told me to practise my arpeggios and I . . ."

"Do as I say, Louisa. Run along now."

But Bron was unwilling to move and Louisa made little effort to persuade him. Tavy waited miserably while the Mistress urged them both out.

"Now, Octavia," she said at last, closing the door. "I hope, after a good night's rest, you have reconsidered my proposal. Shall we not go together to persuade the bushman to let us care for his baby?"

Tavy shook her head.

"You are still of the same opinion as when I last spoke to you?"

"Yes, ma'am."

The Mistress sighed. She crossed the room, straightening the curtain, then back to the fireplace, brushing away the

142

grevillea flowers that had fallen from the Christmas decorations.

"But Octavia," she said, speaking in a thoughtful voice, "If this bushman is as worthy a character as you think he is, would he not realise, as both you and I do, that his child would be infinitely better cared for here?"

For a moment Tavy thought over what the Mistress had said. "Oh, he is worthy, truly he is, but he loves Joe ever so much and he wouldn't let nobody else have him, not in a hundred years he wouldn't. I mean, if you was in his place, ma'am, would you have let strangers take Master Harry away when he were just a little fellow? And, if you'll pardon me saying it, ma'am, not just strangers but people what you knew wanted to be rid of you."

She watched the Mistress anxiously. Had she said too much? Would her last remark be considered impertinent? To her surprise, the Mistress nodded her head and said, "Perhaps you are right, Octavia. You appear to know the bushman better than I had imagined. We should not interfere and, after all, we must not ignore the fact that the help you were able to give him was, at best, limited by your duties here. Is that not so?"

"Well, yes, ma'am. I wasn't there that much, but I did a lot when I was and you see . . ."

The Mistress held up her hand. "I'm sure you did," she went on. "Even so, it was insufficient for a baby of that age, who should have constant attention. It distresses me very much to think of the child in such conditions, a primitive hut in this dreadful drought, with Aborigines camped nearby, so Harry tells me." She sighed again, shaking her head. "I feel sure, Octavia, that though you are clearly fond of the baby, you will agree with me that the sooner the bushman takes his son where he can have proper care, the better."

But it isn't only Joe, it's Jake too. I don't want to lose them. Oh, I don't want them to go. The words were so loud inside Tavy's head that she glanced at the Mistress, thinking she must have heard.

"My husband and I are firmly agreed that it is out of the question for you to go to the bushman's hut ever again. It will not help matters. Any assistance you give him will only delay his decision to seek better conditions for the baby. Besides, it would be most imprudent. You must be sensible and try to forget all about the baby. Do you understand?"

"I can't forget him, ma'am."

"Not immediately. But these things soon pass." She smiled at Tavy gently. "Now, Octavia, I want you to promise me that you will not go beyond the orchard in future; stay away from temptation, stay away from the hut."

I can't promise, Tavy thought. I can't because I would have to break it.

"Well, Octavia?"

The door opened and Louisa came in, followed by Bron. "It is no use, Mama. Bron doesn't want to go for a walk." She knelt beside the dog, who sat just inside the door with his tongue hanging out. "He's too hot, poor old boy, aren't you?" She stroked his head. "Anyhow," she added, standing up and crossing to the piano, "it is time for my arpeggios." And she sat down on the stool and began to play.

"It's my day off, Lily," Tavy said, "and what I do is none of your business."

"But the Mistress told you not to go down there any more," Lily said swatting at the flies buzzing round the dairy window.

It was early Sunday morning and Mrs. O'Rourke had sent them to collect milk and butter for breakfast. Tavy fitted the lid back onto the milk churn. "I never promised her, though," she said. It was true. How annoyed Louisa would be to know that she had reappeared at just the right moment! "Anyway," she added, "I didn't tell you I was going, did I?"

"Oh, come on, Tavy, I know you're planning to hop off down there to see that baby. Why not say so?"

"Because, if you don't know, Lily, you can't tell no one, can you?"

"Well, if you go, you'll be downright stupid. Master Harry says there's Abos near the creek and they can be real nasty when there's drought like this, honest they can. It's so hot anything can happen."

"Then it can happen to Joe too, can't it?" Tavy said, picking up the churn and going out. Arguing with Lily just made everything more difficult because she knew what Lily said was true. Besides, she hated to disobey the Mistress, who had been kind and understanding. But it was four days now since she had been to the hut, four days of wondering and worrying, four nights too, staring into the dark, unable to sleep. She had kept on remembering Lily's words, 'it's so hot anything can happen', and the Abos were close, they could be 'real nasty'. Once or twice she had crept outside to look up at the stars. "Keep Joe safe," she had whispered. "Keep Jake safe too." In the mornings there were black rings under her eyes.

"You look a wreck, Tavy," Mrs. O'Rourke had said. "Stop pining for that baby and eat up, girl. You'll be fading away, to be sure you will."

"I'm not hungry," Tavy had said. But what about Joe? Was Jake managing to feed him? Had he enough food with no chance to hunt and no water to spare for the vegetable patch? The questions went round and round in her head. Somehow she had got to go back to the hut.

But it would not be easy. There was something else as well she had almost forgotten. Sam. As far as she knew, he had never discovered her secret way to the hut, going behind the hedge at the end of the paddocks and lately he seemed to have given up watching her suspiciously. He had never been friendly, scarcely spoke to her at all, but occasionally, when she wished him good morning, he would respond with a grunt and a nod of his head. It would be different now, now that he knew she had been looking after that bushman's child. And slipping down there without him finding out. Stickybeak Sam, who prided himself on never missing anything that went on round Tallangatta. He would not let her pass by unnoticed again. But that was

145

exactly what she must do.

In the heat of the day, a Sunday at that, she should be safe enough. The danger was that Sam would know it was her afternoon off and, when dinner was over, he would be watching for her. If only, if only I could think of a way, she thought, as she knelt in the drawing room at Sunday morning prayers. The stifling heat seemed to wrap her round, sweat streamed down her body, there was no air to breathe. If only, if only . . . "Spare us, good Lord" . . . The Master's voice droned through the prayers. At last they stood up. There was shuffling and sighing as Louisa went to the piano. The music started, harsh twanging notes, louder and louder inside her head. She felt dizzy and sick, the music roared, thundering darkness pulling her down.

"There now, dearie, you're all right."

The music had stopped. Tavy opened her eyes. A round face hung over her like a crimson moon. It was Mrs. O'Rourke.

"Let me see to her," said a voice. The Mistress was looking down at her now, her face full of concern. She smoothed Tavy's forehead. After a moment, she held something under Tavy's nose. "Breathe in deeply, Octavia," she said. It smelled sharp and strong, like ice in her head. What was she doing on the floor, with everyone staring at her?

"Did I . . .?" she started.

The Mistress smiled and patted her arm. "It's the heat," she said. "You will soon feel better."

"Mama." Louisa's voice came from across the room. "Mama, I feel most unwell."

"Oh my poor lamb," the Mistress said, rising quickly.

Tavy tried to sit up. Her stomach heaved. "Stay there, Octavia," the Mistress said.

"But ma'am," Tavy said, "I'm going to be sick."

"Trust you, Tavy," Lily said. "Could have done without spending the rest of the morning scrubbing that carpet, in one bucket of water too. That's all I were allowed! The

146

smell! Phew!" She held her nose and turned her eyes to the ceiling.

"I'm ever so sorry, Lily, truly I am," Tavy said. "Oh, I do feel ashamed, being sick and all as well as everything else what's happened." She rolled over, hiding her face in the pillow.

"Don't take on so. You only fainted. Mrs. O'Rourke says it often goes with a good throwing up. Besides, you didn't make half such a fuss as that Miss Louisa. You've never heard such a carry on in all your life, and she didn't even pass out proper like you. I reckon it was just a sham because you was getting all the attention but the Mistress is still clucking round her like a mother hen. Not much chance she'll come and see you. She says I'm to tell you to stay on your bed all afternoon. You're to have a good sleep and I'm to keep an eye on you. So you'd best forget about flying off to you know where." She pulled a few curls from under her cap, fluffed them up with her hair brush and studied the result in the mirror. "Anything you want before I start serving dinner?" she asked, opening the door.

"No," Tavy said. "I'm all right now." She looked directly into Lily's eyes. "Just leave me alone, please, Lily," she said.

Lily nodded slowly. "If that's what you want." And, with a wink and a grin, she turned and ran off.

It was, in fact, all she wanted. Now, while Lily and Mrs. O'Rourke were busy, the family in the dining room eating their dinner and, with a bit of luck, Sam eating his for he would not expect her to be free yet, she could slip down to the hut. The only risk was that Lily might split on her. But Lily had winked. She had definitely winked.

Tavy got up quickly and put on her dress. Her head was swimming and her legs felt limp. Don't be such a jelly, she ordered herself in an Aunt Lavender-like manner and, picking up her boots, she padded barefoot across the court-yard, skirting the garden, to the orchard gate. There was nobody about, but she ran all the way, snatching a few oranges for Joe as she passed, then over the fence down the far side of the hedge and into the bush, crackling over the

147

dry twigs. The creek was little more than a trickle now. It could not last for many more days.

She saw Jake as soon as she came out of the trees. He was walking away from her along the side of the hut.

"Jake." Her voice sounded weak. "Jake."

He swung round and, as she ran towards him, a huge grin creased his face. He held out his hands and gripped her shoulders. "You've come back then," he said.

For a moment, Tavy could not speak. She just stared at him and her whole body seemed to turn to water. She leaned against him, her head reeling. "Oh Jake," she gasped. Then she pulled away. "I'm so glad to see you!"

Jake nodded. "Glad to see you, girl. They let you come?"

Tavy shook her head. "There'll be trouble if I'm caught, but I had to see you. Is Joe all right?"

Without waiting for an answer, she ran on to the front calling, "Joe, Joe." He came crawling through the door when he heard her voice. She flung down the oranges and picked him up, with Wolf bounding round her at the end of his rope.

"Gub," said Joe, beaming.

"That's his new word," Jake boasted, following her round.

"Oh Joe, you're so clever." Tavy hugged him tight. Then she looked anxiously at his small grubby face. "Have you had enough food?" she asked Jake.

"No meat," he said. "Couldn't leave Joe to go hunting, with Abos so close. Goat ain't giving much, grass is too dry. We need rain real bad." He glanced at the sky and shook his head. "No sign of a break. Reckon I'll have to find water some other place. Could be some left in Tea Tree Creek, south of here. It's a long haul to fetch it but we've got to have water."

"I'll stay with Joe if you want to go now."

"Yep. Keep an eye on the dog. He's not had much tucker, poor devil, and he's wild for water. But don't give him more'n a mugful. Can't spare it."

Tavy nodded. "Poor Wolf," she said, and the dog looked

up, whining. "He has got thin."

"You be all right on your own with him?"

It was the first time Jake had asked her that. Was he thinking of the Abos? But if she questioned him, he would guess she was afraid and he had to go.

"We'll be fine," she said. "Won't we, Joe?"

She stood watching, with Joe in her arms, while Jake saddled the horse. "Take care," he called as he rode away. She waved till he was out of sight then, for a moment, she stayed where she was, staring into the trees.

She kept Joe inside while she tidied and swept, feeding him on segments of orange to quench his thirst. Every so often, she went to the door, shading her eyes. The clearing lay silent, incandescent with heat. Wolf gazed at her pitifully, his yellow eyes pleading. She poured him a dribble of water and he went on lapping at his dish long after it was empty. Joe was restless, crawling into everything, protesting when Tavy pulled him out of the hearth or away from the door. She closed it for a while, but it was dark and airless so she opened it again and put Joe in his cot, with a tin and a spoon. He banged them together in a bored kind of way, then grizzled till she lifted him out. "Gub," he said, pleased to be free.

Then Wolf started barking, staccato sounds stabbing the air. Tavy carried Joe to the door. Wolf was tugging at his rope, straining towards the trees in short frantic jerks. There was a figure in the shadows, then she saw another; yes, there were several, facing her motionless, dark on the trees. She went back inside and put Joe down on the floor. She must stay calm. After all, the Abos were only watching the hut. They were not doing any harm. It was best not to think about it, keep busy. She would mix up some damper so that Jake could bake it later on when he lit the fire. She concentrated on kneading the dough, shaping it into a flat round cake.

Wolf kept on barking. She wished he would stop. It was like a hammer being banged in her head. Then she heard something else, a faint cry from outside. She looked round.

Joe? He had gone. She dashed out past Wolf, calling, "Joe, Joe." He was in the middle of the clearing, lying face down, howling. When she picked him up, she noticed a small red patch on his thigh. She touched it with her finger tip and he screamed sharply. He must have been stung, she thought, hurrying him into the hut. She cradled him in her arms, murmuring "There, there, lovey. Soon be better. Don't cry so." But Joe did not stop and, when she laid him on the bed to examine his leg more closely, he arched his back, stretching out his arms and legs, his face contorted with pain. What could have stung him — a wasp, mosquito, an ant perhaps, or was it a spider or even a snake? "There's brown snakes round here what can kill you," Lily had warned. "So can red-back spiders and funnel-webs." Supposing it was one of those. "Oh, Joe," she whispered desperately.

It was her fault. She should have been watching him. How could she have let him crawl out like that? She squeezed an orange into a mug and held it to his mouth, but he twisted his head away so that the juice trickled down his neck. He cried more than ever, so she walked him up and down, patting his back, her panic growing. If only Jake would come back. He would know what to do. Then suddenly she thought of the lotion he had bought at Burrawong Creek. How stupid of her not to have remembered it sooner! She laid Joe down again and fetched it from the shelf next to Jake's rum bottle. 'APLY to WOOND' the label said. Yes, this would help. She pulled at the stopper. It did not move. She tried repeatedly, twisting it in her sweaty hands, holding it with a cloth to get a better grip; she tugged with her teeth, poked at it with the tip of a knife. Nothing would shift it. Joe was still wailing, wearily now. She sat, rocking him in her arms, bending close to him, whispering, "Dada home soon, Dada home soon," over and over, praying that he would be. Gradually, Joe's sobs subsided, his thumb went to his mouth, his breathing steadied and silence fell on the clearing again.

"Where's the dog?"

Tavy's head shot up. Jake stood at the door, streaked with dust, his gun in one hand, a water bottle in the other. She had not heard him come back. She must have dozed off.

"The dog," Jake repeated, glancing round. He propped his gun against the wall and put the bottle on the table.

"He was outside, barking. There were Abos . . ."

"He's gone."

"What!"

"Bust his rope." He cursed under his breath, breaking off as he noticed Joe on her lap. "What's up with Joe?"

"It's his leg." She moved Joe gently so that Jake could see. Joe moaned and turned his head, but he did not wake. The patch looked bigger, angrier now. Jake tossed off his hat and crouched beside Joe. He smelled powerfully of horse and sweat.

"Is it a snake bite?" Tavy asked anxiously. "He's been crying and crying."

"Not a snake, ain't no fang mark. Did you see anything?"

"No. He crawled out when I was busy. It was my fault, Jake." She hesitated, on the edge of tears, then, taking a breath, she went on. "It was only a little mark at first, but it seemed to hurt him. I tried to put on some of that lotion, but I can't get the stopper out."

Jake wiped his palms on the seat of his trousers and tried to open the bottle.

"Damn thing's stuck," he said grimly.

He picked up a knife and tapped the neck of the bottle with the back of the blade. Then he tried again. "Ah, that's got it."

He knelt beside Joe, tipped some lotion onto his finger and dabbed it onto Joe's leg. Joe woke with a start, screaming and struggling in Tavy's arms. "Steady, son." Jake dabbed on more. He glanced up at Tavy. "This stuff's real good."

She nodded, blinking hard and biting her lip. Joe's cries were like a knife in her heart.

"Here, give him to me," Jake said, taking Joe. He held

151

him in his arms, rocking him gently till gradually Joe became calmer. "He'll sleep now," Jake said. He laid him in his cot and stood gazing down at him. Tavy looked at his back view, his big shaggy head, his dusty clothes. She wanted to run and hold on to him, to let him comfort her, but his thoughts were with Joe. She must not interfere. He had so many troubles and now this had happened and it was her fault. She longed to tell him how wretched she felt, ask him to forgive her.

"Jake, I . . ."

He did not move and her courage failed.

"I'll have to go."

He turned round, his face in shadow. She picked up her boots and went to the door then, on an impulse, she ran to him. He put out his arms and drew her close and for a moment she was pressed against him. He held her away, wiping the tears from her cheeks with his roughened hands.

"Don't worry, girl," he said. "Joe will be all right."

Chapter Thirteen

"Dashing away with a smoothing iron, he stole my heart away."

There was someone singing. Tavy struggled to wake up.

"It was on a Monday morning . . ." It was Lily's voice. She was standing at the mirror brushing her hair. "Woken up at last," she said. "Well, get on and dress. You've finished your fainting fits now, Tavy Finch. There's a mountain of washing to do before breakfast."

Tavy sat up holding her head. She felt dazed. "What happened?"

"What happened!" Lily echoed. "That's good coming from you. Oh, I knew you'd fly off to that baby of yours, but you needn't have stayed that long! I never told so many lies in me life. 'How's Tavy?' says Mrs. O'Rourke; 'Is Octavia resting?' " Lily did a passable imitation of the Mistress. "Lucky for you there was such a to-do going on over Louisa or you'd be in right trouble. And so would I!"

"Thanks, Lily," Tavy said in a contrite voice. "Thanks ever so much."

"Oh, don't mention it," Lily said airily. "Anything to oblige." She glanced at the cup on Tavy's chair. "Managed your tea all right, I see."

Tavy had found it when she got back and had drunk it gratefully, then, with enormous effort, she had dragged off her dress and fallen into bed.

"You was dead to the world last night," Lily said. "I tried to rouse you to tell you the news but . . ."

"What news?"

"There's a couple of rams missing from the paddock by the wool shed. Garrity came to tell us while we was having supper. He reckons it was Abos because there weren't no carcasses lying around, but Sam saw the bushman's dog in there chasing them and he's sure it was the dog what killed them. He says the Abos came and pinched the carcasses later on."

Tavy stared at Lily, her hands to her face. "Oh Lily, that's dreadful."

"Don't see why you're taking on so. They wasn't your rams."

"What happened to the dog?"

Lily shrugged. "Ran off, I suppose. It was late, getting dark."

"Does Master Harry know?"

"He knows now. Sam came to tell him after supper, just when Harry and me was — well, getting down to it. You'd

153

think the old fool could have waited till morning," she added irritably.

"What did he say?"

"Who? Come on, Tavy, do hurry up."

"Master Harry. What did he say?" Tavy persisted, buttoning her green and white dimity.

"Don't know. I waited for ages but he didn't come back." She pulled a face, then she grinned. "Don't you worry though, we'll make up for it tonight."

Lily tipped a bucket of water into the wash tub, slopping it over the floor. "Oops," she giggled. "Mustn't waste it."

Tavy watched the soap bubbles dissolve into scum, ignoring Lily's prattle. All this water just for washing clothes while Jake had to ride miles for a bottleful. And now Wolf had killed two rams. Well, that was Sam's story. Garrity reckoned the Abos had done it. What about Harry? Would he believe Sam? She tried to remember what Lily had said but there was one thought in her mind that eclipsed all else. Joe. She had to see him and see him soon.

"Another scorcher," Lily said as they pegged the washing on the line.

Tavy looked up at the deepening blue, feeling the sun hot on her face. Let Joe be better, she pleaded silently to the sky. Let Joe be better. The words went on and on in her head.

She sat silent at the kitchen table. Let Joe be better.

"Come on, Tavy." Mrs. O'Rourke tapped her plate. "You're not eating your breakfast."

"I don't really feel hungry." Let Joe be better.

Then there was family breakfast to lay. She followed Lily to the dining room with a heavy tray, taking her time to set out the cups, saucers, plates, spoons. Before she had finished, Lily had gone off to the dairy to fetch butter and milk. Tavy propped her tray by the dresser and went back along the passage to the door. The courtyard was empty. She ran across, turned a corner, glancing about her — no one in sight — then on to the garden, skirting the edge to the orchard gate. As it clicked shut behind her, she heard something move. She swung round. Sam stood in the sheep pens watching her, a grinning mouth beneath the brim of his hat. For a second they faced each other, then Tavy fled. But he had caught her at last.

"Joe? How's Joe?" She flung herself at Jake, gasping for breath.

"Steady, girl." He held her shoulders.

"Let me see him." She pulled away and ran into the hut. Joe lay on his back, sleeping. His face was pale, there were dark shadows under his eyes and his leg — she drew in her breath. The patch had spread; it was swollen and red. She turned to face Jake who had followed her in, clenching her fists to gain control of herself.

"Take a few days," Jake said slowly. "He's been drinking water. Lotion's good too, helps a bit."

Tavy nodded.

"Ain't no more milk," Jake said. "Reckon the Abos took the old goat."

Then Tavy remembered. "Wolf? Is he back?"

"Yep, not long since. Put him on the far side, out of the sun."

Tavy went to the door. Wolf was lying under the trees. He stood up when he saw her and tugged at his rope. She turned back to Jake. "He killed two rams."

"What?"

"Sam saw him chasing them in the paddock. He says Wolf killed them."

Jake swore through his teeth and shook his head. He crossed the clearing, untied Wolf and led him over towards the hut. Wolf was whining excitedly, his yellow eyes wild. His fur was matted with blood and dust.

"We'd better wash him off," Tavy said. "If Master Harry sees him like that . . ."

"He'll shoot him now, howsoever he looks. Can't spare no water. Got to go back for some more." He prodded Wolf with his boot. "Need some place to hide this brute. God knows where."

Tavy tried to think. Jake's bed? Not for Wolf. In the privy? She looked up suddenly. There was a steady clop of hoof beats coming closer. She turned and darted into the hut just as Harry rode out of the trees with a gun across the saddle.

She saw him dismount, stride over to Wolf, aim his gun and fire. The dog dropped to the ground. Jake made an angry noise in his throat. Harry stepped up to him.

"I warned you, Bushman. Your dog killed two breeding rams. My stockman saw him do it."

Jake flung down Wolf's rope, glaring at Harry. "Your stockman," he growled. "He'd tell any damned lie to get rid of me. You reckon what he says is true!" He gave a bitter laugh.

"Watch your tongue, Bushman. I won't hear slander against my stockman. His word is good enough for me." He rubbed the handle of his gun. "By the way," he went on with cool nonchalance, "he also tells me that you have one of our servant girls here again."

Tavy drew back, biting her fists. So Sam had not wasted any time. She felt sick with fear and her legs were shaking. She heard Harry's voice, menacing now. "Send her out, Bushman. She's not your property, you know."

"Not yours neither." Jake was almost shouting now. "She's free, that's what. She can do as she likes, not what you orders."

"Send her out, Bushman," Harry repeated threateningly.

Tavy stared round desperately. It was pointless to hide. She went to Joe's cot. He was still asleep, his breathing quick and shallow, his bright hair dark with sweat. There were footsteps outside. She touched Joe's cheek. He opened his eyes.

"Gub," Tavy said. Joe blinked. "Gub, Joe."

The footsteps came up behind her, a hand gripped her shoulder. She twisted suddenly, ducking under Harry's arm, running towards Jake, but her arm was grabbed from behind.

"Let me go," she cried, struggling to get free.

Joe started to wail, a small weak sound. As Harry dragged her outside, she saw Jake coming nearer. He swung his fist. Harry ducked, sticking out his foot and Jake hurtled forwards, sprawling on the ground. Tavy felt herself seized and lifted. She was lying across the horse, smelling hot leather and sweat. Then Harry swung himself into the saddle and heaved her round so that she was sitting in front of him between the reins. She caught sight of Wolf's body lying by the door, of Jake running, running, trying to catch up. But Harry urged the horse forward, faster, away, cantering quickly through the trees.

Harry rode back to Tallangatta the long way round, up the winding track to the main gate. It was the way that Tavy had never been though she scarcely noticed, pounding along with dust in her eyes and the white hot sun burning her head. There was anger burning inside her too, for her fear had changed to anger now. What right had Harry to treat her like this, a bit of Campion property? Jake had stood up for her. "She's free," he had said. But in Master Harry's eyes she was only a servant, not even a pretty one, just skinny and plain. He was Harry Campion, rich and successful, who could give everyone orders, shoot Jake's dog, with only old Sam's word as evidence. Poor Wolf, she had grown quite fond of him. Then, one crack of Master Harry's gun and he was dead. She could feel Harry's breath down the back of her neck and she tried to wriggle out of his grasp, digging her elbows into his chest.

"Keep still," he ordered, spurring the horse into a gallop so that she had to cling on to the saddle to prevent herself being jolted off.

When they reached the front steps of the homestead, Harry dismounted and stood holding the reins while Tavy slid to the ground with her dress all hitched up. She noticed him glance at her legs before she had pulled down her skirt and she stood on the steps while he secured the horse, keeping aloof, avoiding his eye. Then he took her by the wrist and led her along the passage to the study.

As he opened the door, the Master looked up from his desk and frowned.

"I found her down with the bushman, Papa," Harry said. "Sam saw her go."

The Master nodded. For a moment he regarded Tavy sternly, then he turned to Harry. "Send your mother to me," he said.

"Very well." Harry paused as he went out. "Incidentally, Papa, I dealt with the dog."

"An unfortunate necessity," the Master said and returned to his books.

Tavy stared at her dusty boots, listening to the sound of the Master's nib scratching over the paper, trying to keep her anger alive, trying to keep her thoughts off Joe. Then the door opened and, with a rustle of skirts, the Mistress came in. Tavy did not look at her because she was afraid there would be sadness in her face. She had the feeling that the Mistress was a little bit fond of her and, after all her patience and understanding, it must seem to her that besides being disobedient, Tavy had been ungrateful. She had lost the green beads, her Christmas present, rejected the offer to have Joe at Tallangatta and this time she had neglected her duties, running off on a Monday morning when there was work to be done. Of course she could never have stayed away from Joe, nor from Jake either the way things were now, but she listened unhappily while, in a grave voice, the Master said, "Octavia, my wife and I are exceedingly distressed by your behaviour. After all the consideration we have shown you, your repeated lack of co-operation is hard to believe. It cannot and will not be allowed to continue. You will remain in your room for the rest of the day. I shall speak to you again when we have had time to make a decision about your future."

Tavy stood at the window staring out at the bleached grass,

the heat shimmering on the laundry wall, the patch of deep blue above. It was as if the sun had drained all the colour from the earth and concentrated it in the sky. She turned away and sat on the bed. It seemed hours since the Mistress had escorted her here, closed the door firmly and gone away. Lily had not come in at all, though from time to time Tavy had heard her outside shuffling about, humming to herself. It was like being in prison, with Lily as a warder keeping guard. The Master had said she was to stay here for the rest of the day. What after that? What would the decision about her future be? A month's notice like Tom Grundy at Cadogan Square? It was a long time since she had thought of Tom. He hadn't cared when he was dismissed. Would she mind? Where would she go? There was only one place she wanted to be and that was with Joe. She sighed miserably and propped her head in her hands. No, she must not let herself think about Joe because she would only start to cry. Besides, it was not only Joe she wanted to be with. Now she knew clearly how she felt about Jake, she wanted to be with him as well.

The door opened and Lily came in, carrying a tray. She gave Tavy a reproachful look as she put it down beside her.

"Mrs. O'Rourke says you're to eat every scrap and no nonsense." She turned to go.

"Lily, is it . . ." Tavy began.

"The Mistress told me not to talk to you. You're supposed to be contempulating the error of your ways."

"What's that mean?"

"Contempulating the error of your ways," Lily repeated. "Well, it were some such word. And I'm not talking to you anyway, I just told you." All the same, at the door she paused. "It's no good you thinking of hopping off again neither because I'm to keep an eye on you and report you if you misbehave." With a sharp nod of her head, she went out.

Tavy looked at the tray. There was a mug of tea and three slices of bread and dripping, punishment diet. Well, she didn't want it anyway, except for the tea. She could save the bread for Jake, though it was water he needed most. She went to the washstand and looked in the jug. It was empty. Lily had poured all the water into the bowl and left the soap at the bottom. I'll ask her to fill up the jug, Tavy thought, then I can carry it down to Jake. If I ever manage to get away. But I must. I must see Joe. Poor little Joe. She couldn't keep him out of her mind any longer.

He had been worse this morning. There was no doubt of that, whatever Jake said about the lotion being good. It had not helped yet. Joe's small face had looked pinched and drawn; there were those strange dark circles round his eyes and his leg — oh, just to think of it made her wince — it was so swollen now, poisoned and dark. She felt a sob rise in her throat and she flung herself on the bed, weeping for Joe, weeping for Jake alone at the hut with so many troubles and her whole body ached to go to him.

After a while, she got up and went to the mirror. Her face was streaked with dust and tears and her hair hung down in wispy strands. She went to the washstand and rinsed her face in the bowl. Then she unpinned her hair and brushed it smooth. It was pointless, she knew, for her face would be dirty, her hair tangled, long before she was likely to see Jake again. But at least it made her feel better, helped her to make up her mind. She studied her improved reflection in the mirror. You, she told herself firmly, are going back to the hut.

The question was when. She paced up and down the room, thinking about it. The sooner the better, of course, because Joe was growing weaker all the time, his leg was getting worse, Jake had no water . . . Stop it! she ordered herself, fiercely. It was no good getting tearful again, then blundering out and being caught. This time they might tie her up or nail a bolt across the outside of the door. She would have to choose her moment carefully. Perhaps while Lily was serving supper and the family was in the dining room. There was still the risk that Sam would be watching for her, but she would just have to chance it. What time was it now? She went to the window and leaned out. The sun

160

was no longer overhead, though the sky still seemed to radiate heat, a deadening heat, powerful and hushed. If only there was a breath of wind. She turned round as the door swung open and Lily came in.

"Phew!" She kicked off her boots and flopped onto her bed. "It's so hot! Garrity says it's the hottest he can ever remember since he come to Australia."

"Lily," Tavy said, hoping she would have forgotten the talking ban. "Can we have some more water?"

"What?" Lily did not move.

"Water — the jug's empty. Please will you fetch some?"

"Not a chance. We're not allowed no more till tomorrow. The Master's worried about it running out. You'll have to make do with the slops." She sat up and frowned at Tavy. "I had to do the dinner dishes with one bucketful and it were leg of mutton, all greasy. I could have done with some help, I can tell you," she added accusingly.

Tavy shrugged. "I'm ever so sorry, Lily, but I didn't choose to . . ."

"I'm not talking to you," Lily said, remembering at last. She went to the mirror and fiddled with her hair, singing pointedly. "Well," she said after a few moments, "I suppose I'd better get back to work. There's no peace for them as behaves themselves. It's the wicked what has a nice loaf about."

"I'd love to change places," Tavy said longingly. "It's ever so stuffy in here."

Lily gave her a sideways look. "Hopeful, aren't you? And it's no good you getting ideas about having a breather when it's supper time either because the Mistress has ordered cold collation and they'll help themselves. So I'll have my eye on you, Tavy Finch, all the time."

Tavy sighed deeply. She would just have to wait, go down in the dark when Lily was asleep, finding her way by the light of the moon. But, oh how she longed to escape from this room! She stood in the middle, stretching out her arms, throwing back her head. The rough wooden ceiling was a few feet above, the walls seemed to press in from either side.

She felt trapped, like being on the lower deck of the *Henrietta*, the crowded London streets, the drawing room in the homestead at Sunday prayers. She wanted space, fresh air, the sky. She couldn't last a moment longer . . .

But it was no good. She dropped her arms and lay on her bed. If only she could sleep, then the time would pass without her noticing it. She shut her eyes.

It was getting hotter. She could see the sun right over her head. It was close to her, scorching her face right through to her bones. Looking down, she saw the earth at her feet, blistered and burned, and all around her for endless miles the plain was dying, crumbling to dust. The trees were dry, parched like bones, lifting their arms to the merciless sky. She could hear a sound, a distant cry, and she knew it was Joe. He was all alone, he needed her. "I'm coming," she called, and she held out her arms. She was trying to run but she could not move because the wind was rising, blowing her back, blowing, blowing.

The door slammed shut. Tavy opened her eyes. Lily was moving about the room. Perhaps she was going to bed. Once she had dropped off, it would be safe to go. Lily struck a match and lit the candle on the chest of drawers. It sputtered and went out. She tried again and this time it rose with a thin blue smoke, sending dancing shadows over the walls. Tavy lay still, feigning sleep, listening to the rattle of the door latch, the flap of the curtain as a hot wind blew through the window. She had dreamed of wind — if it was a dream. Now Lily was brushing her hair, swish, swish, on and on. Why couldn't she hurry and get into bed? Her hair would get tangled again while she slept. She was opening a drawer; there was a chinking noise. She was trying on her beads. Through half closed eyes in the candle light, Tavy watched Lily coil them round her neck, lifting her hair, preening herself. Then Tavy heard footsteps coming nearer. They stopped and there were three distinct taps on the door. Lily swung round, her hand to her throat. She took a last look at herself in the mirror, giggling softly as she blew out the candle.

The door opened on a sudden gust and Tavy heard her whisper "She's asleep."

Then a man's voice murmured, " . . . been battening down over at the farm. Sam'll do the rest. Come on, come on." With a loud bang, the door closed and Tavy was alone. Now was her chance, while Lily was with Harry. And Sam— she could hardly believe her luck — Sam was battening down over at the farm. She pulled on her boots and unlatched the door, holding it tight as the wind tugged it back. Dust swirled through the air in the strange half light, stinging her face, blowing into her eyes and mouth. The sky was hidden by lowering clouds, bruised, menacing, driven by the wind. She edged along, keeping close to the wall, head down, her skirts billowing out as she darted across the open spaces between the buildings. A bucket rolled past her, there was a tinkle of glass, a crashing, a tearing, a nightmare of noise. But she did not look round. She edged round the garden, keeping in the shadows. There were lights glimmering in the homestead windows. As she went through the orchard gate, she could hear the wind whistling through the sheep pens. Was it the ghost of Sam, she wondered, as she darted quickly through. Unripe apples rained on her head, twigs and leaves flew from the thrashing trees as she ran past the plums, apricots and oranges, stumbling over the fallen fruit in the grass.

At the edge of the bush, she paused staring in alarm at the tangle of branches flailing above her. Everything seemed to have come alive, whirling and swaying, drawing her into its savage dance. But she must go on. She must get to Joe. As she was tossed from tree to tree, she heard a deep rumble from far away. Thunder. A storm was coming. Yes, she could see lightning too. Yet it couldn't be lightning because it was still there and it came from below her beyond the creek. Perhaps the Abos had moved closer and the light was their camp fire. She stopped for a moment, hanging onto a tree trunk and, as she watched, the light seemed to grow, creeping wider, flickering up. It was not a camp fire. The bush was burning and it was spreading fast, fanned by the wind. The undergrowth was tinder dry. It would only take moments for the flames to reach the hut. "Joe," she gasped, and she was off again, hurtling down the hill, fear speeding her on. She lost sight of the fire as she neared the creek. It was darker now, hard to see the fallen branches, the prickly bushes that tore at her skin. She kept tripping and falling, there was a cut on her face and once, as she struggled to her feet, there was a ripping noise. Her dress, the green and white dimity Jake had admired, was torn. But it didn't matter any more. She crossed the creek and climbed the far bank, then, above the wind and thunder, she heard the sharp crackling of the fire. She could see it now, bright through the trees. It was close to the clearing and, as she ran out into the open, she saw quivers of flame licking the edge of the grass. Jake's horse was not there. Had the Abos taken it as well as the goat?

"Jake! Jake!" she cried, but her voice was weak. "Jake, I'm here."

She ran into the hut, staring wildly round. In the glow of the flames that shone through the door, she saw he had gone. Had he taken Joe? She flew to his cot. He was there.

"Oh, Joe," she sobbed. He looked so ill, so small and, when she lifted him, he seemed almost weightless in her arms.

"It's me, Joe," she whispered, bending over him. His eyes fluttered open, but he did not see her. Holding him close, she ran outside, recoiling for an instant from the heat of the flames. They were only a few feet away from the hut and the wind was driving them rapidly. She fled towards the creek, thoughts whirling through her mind. Where was Jake? Had he gone to fetch water? She must find somewhere safe to wait for him. But the fire was everywhere. Nowhere was safe. And Joe was so weak. He must have proper care. There was only one way to save him. She would take him to Tallangatta. The Mistress would save him, she could not refuse.

There was a crash of thunder, louder now, a shiver of lightning overhead. The storm was close. She hurried on,

164

cocooning Joe in the skirt of her dress, trying to protect him from the scratchy, spiky branches and twigs that seemed to reach out to them in the dark. Suddenly there was a violent roar behind her and a flaring brightness lit up the trees. The hut had caught fire. As she turned to see, she caught her foot, lost her balance and tumbled to the ground. "Joe!" she gasped as she dragged herself to her knees, lifting him to see his face. She stared at him. A drop of rain fell on his head, another and another. She could hear them spattering all round her, but she went on staring at Joe. He was very still. She held him close to her. His breath . . . but she could not feel his breath at all. She touched his cheek, his eyes, his mouth. And then she knew. With a stab of grief, she knew Joe was dead.

Chapter Fourteen

It was dawn when Jake found her. She was lying on her back, sheltering Joe in the crook of her arm. Her clothes were drenched and her face was streaked with dirt and blood. She woke as Jake touched her, staring at him through her tangled hair.

"You all right, girl?" he said.

She sat up slowly, turning to look down at Joe. Jake knelt beside her and picked Joe up. For several moments he gazed down at the small body in his arms. Everything round them was quiet and still. It was as if the whole of the bush was worn out by the storm, battered by the wind and the torrents of rain. Then a little sobbing sound came from

Tavy and she bowed her head to hide her tears. Very tenderly, Jake laid Joe down and, taking both Tavy's hands, he helped her up, holding her near him, stroking her hair. She wept softly, sorrowing for Joe. Last night in the rain, she had cried aloud, a desperate grief till, like the storm, all her strength was used up and she fell asleep with Joe in her arms.

After a while Tavy stopped crying, but she stayed where she was, drawing comfort from Jake, feeling the peace all about her. It was growing light and the birds were beginning to chirrup in the trees. She lifted her head and looked at Jake.

"You did your best, girl," he said. "Maybe it were meant to be this way."

Tavy untied her apron and handed it to Jake. "To put round him," she said.

Jake nodded. He bent over Joe's body, wrapping it carefully. Then, cradling it in one arm, he took Tavy's hand and led her down the slope, kicking aside the fallen branches that lay in her path. Before they had gone far, she could see where the fire had spread up the hill before the heavy rain had quenched the flames. The sodden undergrowth was burned and the leaves had been singed from the bushes and the lower branches of the trees. But, as they came near the creek where the fire had raged in its full fury, the ground was bare, blackened and desolate. Only the gums remained standing, their trunks seared clean of all their bark, gleaming grey-white in the early light. Here and there, fire still smouldered in the hollow trunks of dead trees. Smoke mingled with the vapour that rose from the ground and the air had an acrid, pungent smell of eucalyptus and damp charcoal. Then Tavy heard a trickling sound and she saw there was water in the creek. The ground had been too hard for the rain to soak in and it had run down the banks to the stony bed. Still holding her hand, Jake helped her across, up the far bank and on to the clearing. At the edge she stopped.

"Oh!" she breathed. "How terrible!"

166

There was nothing left, nothing at all but a few charred stones where the chimney of the hut had stood. It had been Jake's home. He had worked so hard, building and fencing. And now it was gone.

"Yep," he said gravely. "That rain came a bit late for me. Fire'd gone right over it when I got back with the water."

"Was it the Abos?" Tavy asked.

Jake nodded. "Their camp fire, I reckon; a spark in the wind."

On the far side of the clearing, Jake's horse was tied to the trunk of a tree. It whinnied and tossed its head as they came across to where the vegetable patch had been. Jake dug the toe of his boot into the roughened soil.

"We'll find a place hereabouts," he said. "Be easier to dig."

He glanced at Tavy and she nodded, understanding. Then he laid Joe's body under a tree and she sat beside it on the damp, black ground, listening to the birds, letting the peace soak into her mind. Jake took the knife he kept slotted through his belt and used it to loosen the soil. scooping it out with his hands. Tavy looked down at the little bundle wrapped in her apron. This was where Joe would lie for ever. Darling Joe, she had loved him so much. She wished she had something to give him, her green beads, a beautiful bunch of flowers. But there were no flowers, not even leaves.

She got up and walked back across the clearing to the creek. There were pebbles at the bottom, bright and clean. She chose them with care, smooth rounded ones that matched in size, and carried them back in her skirt. Jake was waiting for her, bareheaded, and she watched while, with great tenderness, he laid Joe's body in the hollow he had dug. Then he covered it with handfuls of earth and patted the top with the palm of his hand. When he had finished, Tavy knelt down and arranged the pebbles on top in the shape of a cross, and for a while they stood close together beside the small mound. Tavy let the tears run down her face. She did not look at Jake because she sensed that his grief was private and deep. As he turned away and went over to the horse, she noticed him brush his eyes with his sleeve and she waited a moment before she followed him. She stroked the horse's neck and it nuzzled her shoulder with its velvet nose.

"Have to find you some grass, old fellow," Jake said. "Ain't none here."

Tavy stared at the devastation round her. It suddenly seemed like the end of the world; Joe dying, the fire, everything gone.

"Will it ever grow again?" she asked.

"It'll grow all right. Month or so it'll start to show green. Fire like that does the ground good."

Tavy glanced at him in surprise. "So you'll start again? Build a new hut?"

He shook his head. "Not here, not after what's happened."

"Where'll you go?"

He shrugged. "Find a new place. There's plenty of land. It's a big country." He paused for a moment. "Besides," he went on, "Campions don't like me on this run; they've made that plain enough. They're not bad folk. I'm not saying that. They've done pretty well, makes sense for them to want more land." He started to untie the reins from the tree trunk. "You'd best go back there, girl," he said.

For a moment Tavy was silent, thinking. It was morning now. Lily would have discovered that she had escaped. Soon everyone at Tallangatta would know and they would come and find her. She would be in disgrace, punished, dismissed perhaps — unless, without Joe to distract her, they considered she would reform her ways. Without Joe, without Jake too. And if she did not go back, would they miss her? Yes, the Mistress would be distressed to lose her but the Master had seldom spoken to her, to him she was just another troublesome servant. And what about Lily and Mrs. O'Rourke? They'd be bound to miss her help at first, but Mrs. O'Rourke would soon drown any regrets she might have with a draught of physic and all Lily cared about

168

was Harry. Handsome, conceited Harry would certainly not be sorry she had left and Louisa would be downright glad. As for Sam, she could imagine his face under that battered cabbage-tree hat, his toothless grin when he saw the clearing looking like this and realised that Jake had gone for good. He would grin even wider if she had disappeared too. Would they search through the bush for miles around? Perhaps they would think she had died in the fire. The Master would pray for her on Sunday morning. Then they would send to Sydney for another girl, an obedient servant who did not fly off on her own and . . .

She glanced at Jake. He was watching her.

"I'm not going back." Her voice was firm.

"Why not?"

She looked up at the sky. It was rain-washed, clear, boundless space. How could she explain what she wanted to say?

"You see when I'm there I have to do as I'm told. It's always been like that — when I was at Saint Agatha's, in London at Cadogan Square, at Tallangatta — obeying rules, working to order. It's not work what I mind, truly it's not. It's just that, well, I've never felt free, not really, except when I'm here." She hesitated.

"What do you want to do then?"

Tavy took a deep breath. "Jake, will you let me come with you?"

He stared at her.

"I'll work hard, I promise, do anything. I'm strong, truly I am, and I've learned a bit about what it's like living in the bush and . . ." She watched his face anxiously.

"You mean," he said slowly, "you mean you want to be my girl?"

"Yes," she said eagerly. "Yes, that's what I mean. But not just that. It wouldn't be respectable like that. What I mean is . . . "

He came to her and took her hands. "I know what you mean, girl," he said. "You want us to wed, be Mrs. Drummond."

169

A shaft of sunlight came through the gaunt trees, catching his face and it seemed to Tavy to be suddenly different, alight with a quiet gentle joy. He put his arms round her and held her close.

"Reckon that sounds like a good plan," he said. "Reckon you and me could make out pretty well."

Tavy felt as if her heart would burst. "Oh Jake," she said, "I reckon we could."